BANGOR BUS

Pat Jones

ISBN: 1484990366

ISBN-13: 978-1484990360

Cover design by Kit Foster

kitfosterdesign@gmail.com

Condition of sale

CONTENTS

PREFACE

Slight though it was, the weight of the sheep started an imperceptible movement. The quarry edge crumbled away and showered five hundred feet to the pool below. The animal scrabbled ineffectually and plunged, terror stricken, as the ground beneath it vanished.

Beside the stunted rowan tree a man, rifle in hand, broke his cover. To do so was out of character, but the unexpected rock fall had started alarm bells ringing in his head. He established the cause of the avalanche and without emotion, watched the creature struggle hopelessly in the water filled abyss below. Then sinking back into the hollow among the bracken, he raised his rifle to his eye and viewed his surroundings through the telescopic sight.

The mountain sulked, dark and menacing under the early morning sky. Long, thin wisps of rain cloud below the summit, floated outwards like antennae. Without the sun to illuminate her features, the Lady of Snowdon retained her elusive reputation. Over Anglesey, lighter, fluffy clouds splattered an ice-blue canvas. The wind, growing in strength, promised to deliver better weather.

From the valley a narrow strip of tarmac wound its way upwards between isolated cottages and sheep-shorn slopes to another, bigger quarry. An enormous, dull, grey, unhealed wound, its circumference camouflaged occasionally beneath the splendours of rowan or broom.

A red, single deck bus was approaching in the far distance: it began the ascent slowly but confidently, proving to any watching eye that this was a regular event. As it came nearer, the road flattened out along the edge of an escarpment where at each side, scattered, like the detritus from a landslide lay the village.

1. GLASFRYN

The vehicle splashed recklessly through the kerbside puddles and came to a stop outside the newsagents shop in Cwm Wylfa. Jack Lewis, his braces straining beneath a well worn tweed jacket, emerged from the brown painted doorway, heaved his considerable weight up the steps, paused at the top and tipped his cap.

"Bore da Dave... won't be a minute." He glanced down the bus and finding it empty as he expected at this stage of its journey, he turned round and waited expectantly. This time Jim 'Weasley' Williams emerged from the shop, his slight frame hidden behind a thick wad of newspapers which, with an enormous effort, he handed up. Jack Lewis took them from him without apparent effort and sank into the front seat placing them down on the floor beside him. The bus moved off, Dave skillfully avoiding a cat and the dog which followed in hot pursuit across the road. The sound of the hard worked engine echoed between the slate walled houses as the bus left the village and climbed the hill to the Glasfryn council estate where it terminated its journey. Here the road flattened out and turned a hairpin shape at the top of the hill. After circumnavigating the pebble dashed houses which lined both sides, Dave Owen parked alongside a battered looking shelter. Decorated with graffiti over the years, it had a new and vulgar addition this morning.

"That's disgusting," Dave said, reaching down beside the seat for his pipe and tobacco. "Nothin's sacred these days." Then thoughtfully, "Looks like the rain's given over for a time. You'll be glad of that Jack."

Jack looked at the sky above them and then to the top of the mountain above the quarry.

"Looks like it, yes. It was only fine rain earlier on, but wet all the same," he laughed. "They mused silently for a minute or so, while Dave applied a match to the end of his pipe and drew on it. He always welcomed the brief wait at this end of the route and looked forward to his pipe and conversation with Jack. Dave had been driving the Bangor bus for many years. A man happy with his lot and not in the least ambitious, he enjoyed greeting and chatting with the passengers, most of whom he knew well by now. Jack never ceased to amaze him. He walked the mile and a half down to the village every day, collected the papers and taking advantage of a free lift back, delivered them around the Glasfryn area. This he did, in all weathers; quite an undertaking for a man in his seventies. Obviously his girth belied his ability to perform this self appointed task."

He smiled at his friend who was enjoying a rest on the front seat.

"You're a bit earlier than usual this morning," Jack remarked scanning the empty road through screwed up eyes. The bright morning light seemed to bother him these days. Dave pushed up the cuff of his brown uniform jacket and consulted his watch.

"They'll all come out in a minute though," and as if to prove the truth of his words, doors began to open and people spilled out unhurriedly, turning in the direction of the bus. The two men fell into a companionable silence, broken only by muttered greetings as passengers climbed on board and showed their season tickets. After ten minutes, Dave wound down his window and knocked his pipe out on the wing mirror. Jack descended the steps, turned at the bottom and pulled the pile of newspapers towards him. Grabbing hold of the string that bound them he swung his arm and dropped them on the slatted wooden seat in the bus shelter.

"Be seein' you at choir tonight then." He saluted Dave and as the bus pulled away, extracted a number of papers from the pile and set off to deliver them to the nearby houses. This done, he picked up the rest and headed for the narrow, well trodden, track. Threading his way between the potholes that householders had optimistically filled with rubble and cinders, he took his time. The council claimed not to be responsible for the road, such as it was, up to the cottages. Since the quarry had closed ownership of it was an ongoing argument. Breathing heavily, he was each day, becoming more aware of the angina, diagnosed so recently. He patted his pocket where he kept his spray. With that to hand, he would be able to carry on doing the paper round for a fair time yet, he thought.

Jack had worked in the quarry until ten years back when the place had closed leaving most of the men in Cwm Wylfa without work. Feeling lost with so much time on his hands, he had taken upon himself this job of delivering the daily papers to friends and neighbours who lived round about. Apart from two years National Service in the army, he had always been employed at the quarry, clogging his way daily past the cottages to the work sheds beyond.

The men were fit, strong and usually oblivious of the steep climb. They had followed the footpath through rain, hail, sleet and snow, knowing it when it resembled torrent, or mini glacier and when it sprouted fresh green grass and buttercups. Sometimes honeysuckle embraced the walls on either side, throwing out a sickly fragrance and later in the autumn, brambles offered juicy fruits. They walked in two's and three's, singing, joking, mournful, their moods reflecting the story of the quarry, its triumphs and tragedies. Now in his seventy first year Jack plodded daily over all that was left of the familiar route, delivering the Daily Post to people who, like him, remained in limbo between the old and the new way of life.

The council houses behind him were homes to the sons and daughters of his former colleagues, but his own generation still lived mainly in the old quarry cottages. He enjoyed chatting with them as he delivered their papers and it was often well into the morning before he finished. Glancing back he saw a figure run out of the end house and hail the bus. Young Robbie Owen, late as usual. He's a real chip off the old block, he thought and chuckling to himself he remembered the way Robbie's grandfather had earned his reputation.

Every morning the men would pass the house where Will lived, shouting out amusing and often ribald remarks as he failed to appear. They would carry on walking and a slight, wiry figure would emerge from the doorway some few minutes later, throwing a cap on his dark curly hair and a kiss in the direction of his wife. By the time the men arrived at the sheds, Will Owen had caught up with them, bright and breathless, cheerful as ever and ready with endless repartee. Out of them all, he was the merriest and he had a most infectious laugh. Sadly, he claimed the honour to be the first man from the village to be killed in the war.

Jack began to climb the path that was a short cut between the old road and the railway. At one time where it was steepest, steps had been constructed from slate slabs. These days he negotiated them with difficulty because rain and neglect had taken control. Pausing for breath, he turned and surveyed the valley below. Far beyond the shoulder of the mountain, he was just able to make out a tiny red speck in the distance; the second bus of the morning, turning off the main road in the direction of Cwm Wylfa.

Continuing his walk, he reached a small gate which once served to keep sheep off the narrow-gauge railway track. The old metal barrier now hung from one hinge, broken and rusty. The railway lines had long since been removed and the embankment had become rich pasture. Several sheep were grazing there but turned away when they caught sight of him.

Whistling happily he turned right along the track and went through an opening in the slate wall leading to Agatha Jones' garden, brushing past the dripping hydrangea bushes. Folding her newspaper carefully he inserted it into the vertical letter slit behind the tarnished brass knocker. There was a time when she would have died of shame before allowing her front door to present such a shabby aspect. Widowhood, and children far from home, had left her lonely and sad and her house reflected her feelings. He had a loving daughter but who did Aggie have? No family near, that's for sure.

"Bore da Jack," a voice hailed. Jenny Peters plump figure clad in navy anorak and trousers, came towards him, hand extended.

"I'll take my paper, thanks. I'm off to Bangor on the eight forty... meeting Sheila."

"How's the baby?" he enquired.

"Fine now, thank you Jack, out of the incubator and gaining weight. She'll be able to have him home when he's a bit stronger. We're calling at the hospital to see him today." He watched her hurrying towards the path he had just come from and called after her,

"Remember to give Sheila my best."

She waved an acknowledgement and passing by the broken gate, disappeared down the steps towards the bus terminus. He knew Jenny Peters had suffered a lot of anxiety recently on behalf of her daughter's premature son. Funny, how the woman could have three children without trouble then all that bother with a fourth. Still, all was well now.

Ted Edwards slammed his front door shut and buttoning his old tweed jacket across his thick, fawn sweater, walked down the short garden path to join Jack. His ruddy face and shock of grey hair beneath his tweed cap were a familiar and welcome sight. He and Jack had been at school together and had remained friends ever since.

"Morning Jack. Diawl, tis a bit nippy this morning," he pulled his collar close around his neck and stuck his hands in his pockets. The two of them walked along the row of terraced cottages, delivering the papers as they went. Ahead, lay some stone built, detached houses, their pointing emphasised by thick, pale cement, reminding Jack of a cottage in a Hansel and Gretel pantomime. Three windows upstairs and two down with a central door, their symmetry giving each one the look of a dolls house. The two men picked their way carefully, avoiding the puddles and pot holes. Lumps of slate lay haphazardly in their path, testament to the fact that vehicles rarely came this far. The only adventurous drivers were the milkman and the postman. The latter travelled at such speed that everyone assumed he was trying to fly over the rough surface, while the milkman drove deliberately slowly, the bottles rattling ominously in their crates.

"Mumbo, look you, waiting for his milk." Ted indicated the cat sitting on the low wall in front of Mary Jane's house. He stood up meowing and stretched as they approached and while Ted made a fuss of him, Jack said,

"I'll go for the coal," and handing Ted the few remaining newspapers, he picked his way over the broken slate slabs that formed the path round to the rear of the house. Jack always fetched in a scuttle of coal in for Mary Jane because her arthritis was so bad. Ted re-filled it later in the day. Jack rounded the corner, noticing as he did so that the water butt was leaking. He was just making a mental note to do something about it when,

"Ted... quick," he yelled, seeing the blue bundle lying on the path in front of him. Ted hurried as best he could over the rough and slippery slates, worried by the note of urgency. Rounding the corner of the house he saw Jack crouching beside Mary Jane who was lying unmoving, on the ground. He called out,

"Dear God Jack, what's happened?"

2. MARY JANE

Mary Jane Parry had been awakened by the birds at six o' clock as usual. She lay listening for a few minutes. The insistent, repeated shriek of a blackbird suggested that danger was lurking in the feathered world, probably one of the cats from Bryn Farm in search of a tasty breakfast. Mumbo didn't bother with birds these days, like her, he was getting old. A weak, wet looking sunshine filtered through the crack between the faded floral curtains and quickly disappeared again. A chilly draught blew intermittently through the broken pane in the little window. She heard scuffles from the lane outside as some sheep hurried by, and a rumble from the room below as the grandfather clock got ready to strike.

Painfully, for this was the sort of weather which nurtured her rheumatism, she disentangled herself from the feather-mattress, extending a gnarled hand in the direction of her old blue dressing gown. She rubbed the knuckles which were of similar hue and managed to tie the belt around her slight, bony frame. She slipped her feet into a shabby pair of house slippers and with the aid of her walking stick, carefully negotiated the stairs.

She hooked her walking stick over the back of a chair. The back door had swollen with the wet weather so she had to tug hard to open it, finding the procedure painful and difficult. How wonderful it must be, she thought for the umpteenth time, to have an indoor lavatory. Outside a narrow path led to the ‘ty bach’ and the woodpile alongside. The slabs of slate which she could remember her father laying long ago were now islands in an ocean of field grass. The slate wall which bordered the tiny garden was glossy with rain. Patches of lime green lichen glowed luminous on its purple surface.

She pulled her dressing gown close across her chest, retrieved her walking stick and stepped out. The path was very slippery and tufts of the wet grass showered her ankles. By the time she reached the lavatory door her feet were numb. She should have put on her outdoor shoes, but the effort was too much first thing in the morning. She needed to be up and about for a few hours before she was able to bend over to tie shoe laces. As she went inside, a gust of wind disturbed the branches of the rowan tree, causing raindrops to drip and rattle on the corrugated roof. She shivered. Sheep wandering down from the mountain took a short cut over the garden wall and left their droppings on the path.

There had been heavy rain in the night but Mary Jane thought the morning sky promised better weather. She picked a few sticks of firewood from the woodpile to add to those already drying in the kitchen and gathering her dressing gown around her once more, turned back to the house. Halfway along the path, she stepped on a small cushion of moss, her foot skied across its saturated surface and she fell heavily, her stick slithering out of reach, the firewood scattering.

It could have been minutes or hours later. Mary Jane became aware that she was, cold, and wet and her hands and feet were quite numb. She tried to move, to raise herself, but the pain was excruciating. She lay drifting in and out of consciousness, barely aware of the fine drizzle insinuating itself into the fibres of her clothing. It gathered into tiny rivulets on her face and spilled into a hollow on the surface of the slate where she lay. Unfocussed eyes saw the tiny puddle and her muddled mind tried to interpret the picture. Gradually the mist cleared and she saw the glass dome which housed her father's ornamental gold clock. She saw the blue china panels decorated with roses adorning each side, as it stood proud on its velvet stand. Hands reached out and the dome was gently lifted and put on one side. A key was inserted into the face of the clock and her father leaned forward counting as he wound the delicate mechanism. She saw his rugged, handsome face, his tender kindly smile, the thinning grey hair and the briar, unlit as usual. It had been a family joke, but a kind one, for everyone knew that he could not afford many smokes in a week.

Something wet was rubbing against her face; Mumbo. He was bedraggled, with rain spiked fur and dirty paws. He sniffed inquiringly and rubbed against Mary Jane's forehead.

“It's no good Mumbo; I'm stuck here till someone comes.” Mumbo sat down resigned to the situation and began to wash his underside. “Oh Mumbo, I wish you could tell somebody,” Mary Jane began to cry, “I'm so cold.” She tried to move again; perhaps she could pull herself gradually towards the house. It was impossible; she fell back causing the pain to sear through her and render her unconscious again. Mumbo, wandered off in search of attention elsewhere.

A shaft of weak sunlight broke through the clouds and fell across the garden where Mary Jane lay. Part of it lit up the ashen face and brought her back to reality. She felt very ill and hoped someone would come soon. She lay staring at the sky; brilliant blue patches were appearing here and there. Some clouds moved faster than others, reminding her of ballet dancers on a stage. Her mother had taken her to the theatre once, in Liverpool. Entranced, she had watched the ballerinas as they floated in their white dresses across the stage. It was utter magic, another world, far removed from the one to which she was accustomed. The warm theatre made the wind outside a cold and unwelcome change because it blew away the magic and brought back reality. She remembered standing on the draughty station platform listening to the impatient hiss of steam from an engine. There were so many people that she wondered where they might all be going. She couldn't visualise everyone of them doing ordinary things, like going to bed every night. Bed! If only she could get there. She gritted her teeth and bending one knee tried to push herself along on her back but it was no good. Carefully she straightened her leg and tried to turn. This time the pain hit her with such force that she cried out.

A spider repaired its web, suspended between two tall grass stalks. Drops of rain hanging like baubles were dislodged and fell off as it worked. Mary Jane wondered what the time was. The dog at the farm was barking. Could it be greeting Elwyn the milkman? She doubted it, surely too early for him? Now, heavy steps and laughter. Men on their way to the quarry laughing and joking. Soon she would hear the first engine of the day taking its load of slate down to the valley. No, no, she was slipping into the past again. The quarry had been closed for years. It couldn't be workmen, but there were voices. Call out, call for help. The voices and the footsteps came nearer,

"Help me, help..." she attempted to raise herself so that it was easier to call. "Help me," she breathed faintly as the pain enveloped her and she fell back.

3. TO BANGOR

Dave Owen sighed as he applied his foot to the brake and drew up for young Robbie. He remonstrated with the lad, wagging his fore-finger as he spoke.

"One of these days I'll not be stopping, mark you. Beats me why you can't get up in time... young thing like you. Why should I have to stop special like? Tell me that now."

Robbie grinned wickedly and smiling round at his captive audience retorted,

"Come off it Mr. Owen, if I wasn't a good athlete I wouldn't catch you anyway. Leaping on to the bus is good practise for my long jump."

"Y'll make history... first to jump wi'a leg in plaster." The voice from one of the seats caused a ripple of laughter as Robbie quite unabashed took a seat behind Dave. All the way to the village he chatted happily over Dave's shoulder. There was no doubt he was keen on athletics and from the way he spoke was confident of his ability.

"Bet you I get to the Olympics then."

"I'll believe that when I see it. Olympic athletes have to be up early, running miles before breakfast you know, no lying in bed for them." They pulled up opposite the newsagents and a number of people were waiting to board the bus. There were several children who attended the same school as Robbie, Albert the car-park attendant at Happistores and young, attractive, Moira who had just started her first job in the bank. Jim 'Weasley'

Williams called from the shop doorway across the road.

"Drop these off for me will you Dave? Grace Jones is collecting for the hospital library." I never got around to reading many of them. Not likely to now, he laughed. He struggled across the road with two boxes of paperbacks which he rested on the steps of the bus. Then with a lot of panting and puffing he thrust first one and then the other into the space beside Dave and stepped back colliding with an elderly woman.

"Oh sorry Mrs. Elver, I didn't see you there."

"No harm done," she replied climbing into the bus. "Morning Dave, looks like it's clearing up don't you think?" and without waiting for an answer, "Return to Bangor please." She moved down the bus, greeting people she knew and took a seat about halfway down. Her friend Eliza would be catching the bus two stops on and she was very particular where she sat.

Dave Owen watched until Mrs. Elver had taken her seat, then he pulled away from the curb. She was a lovely lady, he thought, always ready with a smile and always so gentle. He was sure she had been quite good looking in her young days and now, although her clothes were not new they were always clean and neat. He remembered some of the stories he had heard about her and her friend Eliza. Now she was a laugh and no doubt about it.

4. LYDIA AND ELIZA

The year had been nineteen thirty four when Eliza Thomas and Lydia Roberts, close friends since starting school, decided one day to seek the bright lights. Chaperoned in their home area by virtue of the fact that their movements around the village were common knowledge, they felt the need to escape. Eighteen years old and used only to serving behind the counter of the local store, they knew they would never see anything of the world unless by their own efforts.

Their parents, bedevilled by bouts of unemployment, no strangers to tuberculosis, leukaemia and a high rate of mortality amongst their younger children, had never aspired to a holiday. So it was that by the time they left school, the girls had never been further than Bangor, a mere twelve miles from the village. Other people had been as far as Llandudno however, and they came back with thrilling stories of theatres, tea-dances, shows on the pier and other delights. One fateful night, full of trepidation, the girls crept from their respective homes, the dawn light illuminating two notes left on kitchen dressers. They carried the few clothes they owned and basic toiletries. Though dressed only in plain cotton frocks both girls had a certain attraction. Lydia's violet blue eyes sparkled in a mischievous, elfin face framed by dark curls, whereas Eliza had a round open laughing face, straight brown hair and large brown, cow like eyes. Used to walking, they soon reached the main Bangor road, where they begged a lift from a passing milk cart. At the railway station they had just enough money for tickets, and were in Llandudno by ten o'clock.

Their excitement took away any initial anxiety, but as they wandered along Mostyn Street amongst the well dressed holiday-makers, they began to feel a little apprehensive. By twelve o'clock, they were distinctly hungry and hadn't any money. The train ticket had cost more than expected, so now they hadn't enough money even for a cup of tea and a bun. Perhaps this adventure hadn't been such a good idea after all. Lydia began to regret the note she had written, knowing the heartache that her mother would feel, but there was to be no going back when she thought of her father's reaction. She couldn't face the inevitable thrashing she would get for 'shaming' him.

"What are we going to do?" She looked at Eliza. "I'm hungry."

"You aren't alone in that," Eliza replied and with a certain confidence announced, "what we must do is find ourselves a job, now. Pulling at her friend's sleeve she turned down a side road which she could see led to the promenade. The hotels are always wanting chambermaids I'm told. Let's go and try our luck." She steered Lydia towards the row of hotels along the sea-front.

"Look at them all, dozens of hotels and they all need staff." Lydia surveyed the curved terrace of hotels facing the bay. They looked so grand, painted in various pastel colours and with their names in large letters over the doors.

"But we can't go to any of these places," Lydia protested throwing out her arms, "they're far too posh." She stopped suddenly, causing two young men who had been immediately behind them to do the same. One of them however was unable to avoid treading on Lydia's heel.

"I beg your pardon. I do hope I didn't hurt you." He bent down to examine her foot as she tried to pull on the shoe he had dislodged. Their heads bumped together and so startled were they at this second collision that they stared at each other for a moment and then burst out laughing. He shuffled a panama hat from one hand to the other and ran his fingers through blonde wavy hair. Hazel coloured eyes squinted at her in the bright sunshine.

"I say, I'm awfully sorry. I don't make a habit of bumping into young ladies you know." He looked at her foot again, "Are you sure you're alright? I seem to have pulled your shoe off."

"And given her a headache into the bargain" chimed in his friend. "I think the least you can do is treat the young lady to an ice cream." Lydia blushing from shyness and confusion was further alarmed.

"Oh it's alright, really it is," she stammered and then recoiled from a severe poke in the ribs from Eliza's elbow. "Well perhaps, if you don't mind... an ice cream would be rather nice." Her smile, she was later told had been sweet enough to melt an ice-berg.

"Well then, let's start off by introducing ourselves shall we? I'm Frank Elver and this is my friend Ivor Cashell." Frank was handsome in white trousers and blazer with red and navy stripes. While he waited for the girls to introduce themselves he played with his panama hat, twirling it round and throwing it from one hand to the other. Ivor stood quietly waiting, and then he said,

"We don't bite, you know." They laughed, gave their names as they shook hands and started to walk together. Lydia found herself walking alongside Frank.

"Shall we go to the Soda-Fountain?" he wanted to know. Lydia felt herself blushing again and fervently wished that she could stop. The man seemed so worldly, so sure of himself and she felt positively timid by contrast.

"If you like... I'm afraid I don't know where you mean. This is our first visit to Llandudno. We only just arrived today," she added in a sudden rush of confidence. He looked surprised,

"Really? I thought by your accent that you must live here."

Lydia liked Frank; she enjoyed talking to him and found herself losing her initial shyness. She was about to explain what she and Eliza were doing, when he took her arm and steered her through a doorway.

"This is the Soda-Fountain, and it's a popular place you'll find. Ivor and I come every day and make utter pigs of ourselves."

Lydia and Eliza looked around in wonder and amazement. They were in a large marble floored room with pink mirror walls, palm trees in tubs dotted here and there and in the very centre an enormous fountain. Hundreds of wickerwork chairs and tables were crowded with people. They were aware of soft music playing in the background and as the two men led them to a table on the far side of the room, they saw that three musicians sat playing on a dais in one corner.

Lydia made her way across the room as if in a trance, for this was the nearest she had ever been to fairyland. It was all so pretty, even the people. She stared open mouthed at a girl in a turquoise dress. It had the deepest neckline possible without being vulgar and her shapely legs were clothed in the sheerest of silk stockings. Even her shoes matched her dress! Rows of gold chains encircled her neck and her blonde hair was sleek and expertly cut. Lydia had never seen anyone so beautiful. She was like someone in a Hollywood film. Yes she looked every bit as glamorous. Her thoughts went back to a film she had seen starring Gloria Swanson. That had been in the

Bangor Plaza on her last birthday.

Gazing around in wonder, she watched the fountain, captivated by the twinkle of lights, amazed to see that they were beneath the water. Automatically she sat in the chair Frank offered, her mind still absorbing the sight before her. The more sophisticated would have noticed that the place was a little shabby and worn in its tenth year, although still popular as Frank had said. A sharp kick on the ankle brought her back to reality and she met Eliza's wink across the table.

"Wake up, dreamer," her friend teased, "answer the question."

"I'm sorry... what..?" She hadn't heard anyone address her, but it became obvious. Ivor said,

"I was just saying, we come here every day for a Knickerbocker glory and we wondered whether you two would like one. We can really recommend them can't we Frank?"

"Yes, rather." Frank agreed and signalled to a waitress. Then he looked at Eliza.

"Lydia tells me you don't live here, that this is your first visit? Where is Cwm...? Whatever it is... the place you come from?"

Between them the girls told their story, how they had left home in the small hours of the morning, how they begged a lift with the milk truck and then explained what they were about to do when Lydia's accident with Frank had occurred. The two men looked somewhat concerned and Frank began anxiously,

"Why were you....? I mean what...?" But before he could finish the waitress stood beside their table, tray in hand bearing four tall sundae glasses. The men licked their lips whilst the girls stared in disbelief. Never had they seen such exotic, edible concoctions. They were afraid to disturb the mouth watering mixture of fruits, ices, sauce and cream. However it was no more than a minute before their hunger reasserted itself and they ate with gusto. Eliza hoping to divert embarrassing questions asked,

"Are you on holiday?" She didn't know what answer she expected but the one she got was a total surprise.

"No, we're at the Arcadia Theatre for the season. We do a musical medley. Ivor sings and I accompany him on the piano," Frank said. "You must come and hear us... hey, come tonight, why not?" Now was the real moment of truth, the time to admit that they had no hotel, nowhere to go. They looked at each other sheepishly and Frank misinterpreted their glance.

"Of course if you have other plans... you can always come another time." The girls felt very embarrassed but had to admit that the reason they were hesitating was because they needed somewhere to live.

"As we told you, we were just about to look for work when we met you. We have to earn some money and we have nowhere to go yet. We were hoping to get a job in a hotel with staff rooms." Now it was the men's turn to glance knowingly at each other, then as though an unseen signal of agreement had passed between them, Frank said.

"We can probably help you....." He looked at Ivor who nodded encouragement, he went on, and, "I hope this won't sound too forward of us, but under the circumstances." Ivor broke in impatiently,

"What he's trying to say is that they need help back stage at the theatre. Nothing special you understand, but someone willing to muck in and sew or repair costumes. Sometimes things need washing or pressing or somebody wants a cup of tea. You could be called upon to do any old job. I don't know what they pay, but there's always the odd tip from some of our star performers. If you like the idea we can take you back to the theatre with us. We have to go soon, for the three o'clock matinee."

Now both girls were really excited. First Llandudno, and now the theatre! Lydia's heart leapt, she didn't need to look at Eliza to know that the adrenalin was surging through her veins too. Soon, chatting excitedly, they were hurrying in the direction of the theatre. Once there, they were taken up some back stairs to a room with 'Costume Shop' written on the door: here they were introduced to a bright looking woman with a mouthful of pins. She was fixing some fringe to a dress on a dummy, removing one pin at a time from between her lips. As soon as she had placed the last pin in the material, she welcomed them, just as Ivor had promised.

"Mrs. Bellamy," she proffered her hand. "I'll certainly be glad of extra help, but the work will be just... well... whatever needs doing. You must understand that. Sometimes costumes get torn, accidents happen, things being spilt on them and that kind of thing. I need people who can muck in and turn their hand to helping with whatever needs doing. Nothing heavy you understand, all mainly to do with costumes or soft props," she smiled, "if you are interested, see old Harris to discuss pay," and she nodded in the direction of a room across the corridor. Excitedly muttering their thanks, the girls hurried out to the room Mrs Bellamy had indicated. The door was open and inside the tiny cubby-hole of a room sat an irritable looking little man in a waistcoat. His thin mouse coloured hair was combed across his balding head and his large nose sat above prominent, tobacco stained teeth. His roll-top desk almost filled the room and the compartments in it were stuffed with papers, pens and all manner of stationery. He didn't wait for proper introductions, but growled out,

"Two pounds fifteen shillings a week: extra when we have a rush job."

It was a small fortune to girls who had previously earned much less. "You will do whatever Mrs, Bellamy asks of you," he said, "but in any case, always make sure you're here at least two hours before each performance and that includes matinees." He dismissed them with a wave of his arm, his eyes fixed on the column of figures on a paper before him.

"I am busy now. You can see me again after tonight's performance."

One problem still remained and that was where to sleep? Ivor and Frank solved this problem too, illegally, but quite happily. They took the girls to their dressing room.

"These cushions laid on the floor will make a bed for one of you," Frank said, "and the other one can sleep on the settee. It will be OK, we know, because we've tried it. We'd been out on the tiles one night and the hotel door was locked when we got back in the small hours!" he and Ivor looked at each other and grinned, recalling their misdemeanour.

"There are lots of old coats and things you can use for bedding, but whatever you do, don't make a noise. We have to keep these rooms locked when we aren't here, and we'll get the boot if anyone finds out that we're using it as a hotel. Just make sure that you have everything you need for the night and then be quiet little mice till we get back in the morning." He cleared his throat ......"Er..., there are facilities here," and he held back a curtain across an alcove at the back of the room. The girls smiled their thanks and the men, murmured,

"Better get going, see you after the performance." Eliza and Lydia hurried to the Costume Shop, where Mrs. Bellamy introduced them to Sheila, Mary and Janet, three girls about their age who were all busy, their nimble fingers sewing a variety of costumes. Mrs Bellamy showed them where and how everything was housed. The room was full of dummies wearing costumes in various stages of creation; a cast iron stove sported at least six flat irons and there were ironing tables, tables with materials, paper patterns and scissors. Two treadle sewing machines stood idle but with costumes draped over the chairs beside them. One wall had small drawers from floor to ceiling like a haberdashers, all clearly marked with bold lettering. RIBBONS – BLUE, RIBBONS – GREEN, RIBBONS – YELLOW Lydia read, her eyes travelling down the first row of drawers. Eliza said,

"Oh look at the flowers," she pointed to a drawer that lay open, spilling out all manner of silk roses.

"Aren't they beautiful?" Mrs Bellamy smiled. "You can stitch them round the hem of this dress. I will show you how we do it."

So the girls began work. They were both handy with a needle and thread, so for the whole of that summer season they made themselves indispensable behind the scenes at the Arcadia. They managed to sleep undetected in the dressing room and after a few weeks, with careful management and a few tips, they were able to move into cheap lodgings a short walk from the theatre. There was never any shortage of work for them because, as Mrs Bellamy had said, accidents happened and skirts got ripped, buttons came off, so there was an unending demand for their needlework. Sheila had to leave when her mother died and she, herself became surrogate to four younger siblings. Janet caught scarlet fever and was in an isolation hospital for several weeks till she recovered. It seemed that Eliza and Lydia had joined the costume shop at just the right time.

Ivor and Frank found the girls pretty indispensable too. In their free time after matinees, they often took them to Payne's tea-dances. With a plethora of costumes in the store, they were never short of pretty dresses to borrow for the afternoon. They didn't ask Mrs Bellamy for fear of a refusal, but they took great care of the things they borrowed. Sometimes they returned to the Soda-Fountain to sample further Knickerbocker glories. Both girls wrote home to allay any fears their parents might have but omitted to say where they were. Occasionally, with their brothers and sisters in mind, they were able to add small amounts of money, although they knew only too well that their respective fathers would scorn anything that smacked of charity. Returning their gift however, would prove impossible without an address to send it to.

Towards the end of September the talk backstage was all about the pantomime season in London, which made the girls feel insecure and worried. Voicing her thoughts to Frank, Lydia was surprised when he squeezed her hand and said,

"There's no need for you to feel insecure my love, surely you know that. Wherever I go, you must come too."

Things happened quickly when she realised that she was in love with Frank. She had never allowed herself to admit it, because he was from such a different background although strangely, he too had run away from home. He considered the army life his father planned, quite out of the question. Mr. Elver would not discuss the matter so Frank quietly left home. After meeting Ivor (who was quite literally singing for his supper as a busker in nearby Chester) they teamed up and found themselves quite popular. Having earned enough money performing at a local festival, they headed for Llandudno and auditioned for The Arcadians. This was their second summer and they were bigger names on the bill. The holidaymakers liked them, finding their songs topical, clever and extremely funny. They planned a great future for their act.

When the season at the Arcadia Theatre came to an end, the theatre closed for the winter, the company broke up and the performers moved on to their various venues. Ivor and Frank were booked at a variety theatre in London's east end till Christmas and then they were to appear in Pantomime at The Apollo, so they moved on to London, quite naturally including both girls in their plans. They all found lodgings in a small hotel and while the men were rehearsing, the girls looked for work backstage. Although they could show the excellent references which Mrs. Bellamy had provided, the Shoreditch Theatre did not need any extra staff. After a few days Lydia found work with a ladies' boutique, where she was responsible for fitting and finishing. Eliza flitted from one job to the next, first in a cafe, then a sweet shop and finally ending up as an assistant matron at a local boys 'school. Her friendship with Ivor began to grow stale and inevitably they drifted apart. She had an affair with one of the school teachers, the first of many flirtations and it soon became obvious that when any man became seriously interested in her she broke off the relationship, spent a few weeks being thoroughly miserable and then waited for a new romance.

"Marriage!" She would spit out the word with a vehemence that frightened Lydia. "You won't get me making that mistake... I've seen enough to know it's not for me."

"Frank and Lydia were married the following spring. Her mother would have liked to attend the ceremony, but her father had still not forgiven her for leaving home, so he forbade his wife to attend. Her siblings were not given the opportunity. Frank found a tiny, semi-detached house in the Harrow area, although small, it was modern with more facilities than Lydia had ever expected to own. She was very happy looking after their dear little home, her adorable husband and their mutual friend and lodger. Ivor lodged with them more for convenience than anything else. It made it so much easier for Frank to work with him on new songs. Ivor came from a large London Welsh family where babies and young children abounded, but he showed no sign of settling for a similar life. However when young Ralph arrived on the scene, he informed Lydia that he was well qualified to be their resident baby sitter.

Life changed dramatically at the end of 1939 when the outbreak of war interrupted everything and Frank and Ivor were called up, each of them signing on for the navy. That same day Eliza appeared on the doorstep. Lydia barely recognised her at first, they had not seen each other for over a year and suddenly out of the blue, she stood there smiling, fit and happy in her A.T.S. uniform.

"Can you get someone to watch the babe?" she asked. "This calls for a bit of a knees up." The four of them, with an easy familiarity wandered round to a local pub, where they exchanged news and enjoyed jokes and laughter as of old. Not wishing to keep their friendly, baby-sitting neighbour too long from her bed, Frank and Lydia said goodbye and returned home, leaving Eliza and Ivor together, like old times. This revived a certain affection and they met off and on when their leave coincided during the following years.

Lydia made the best she could of her life at home without Frank, always waiting eagerly for his next leave. It was sad that he couldn't see young Ralph's first steps, hear his first words and be there in the evening to read a bedtime story. The child was the image of his father and even had the same placid temperament. Lydia took comfort from knowing that she wasn't alone. There were many like her, some with several children to care for and others with elderly parents to look after as well. Frank was home on leave for three days and caring for her like a mother hen, anticipating the birth of their second child in three weeks. They enjoyed three evenings cuddled together on the settee by the fire, while they discussed what names they might choose for the next addition to the family. She would cherish forever the memory of those few days.

"Make the most of the chance to rest while I'm here," he admonished, when she insisted on preparing a roast dinner, cooking the half chicken a kindly neighbour had shared with her, a rare treat in those days of rationing. All too soon the three days passed and with Ralph in her arms at the gate, she waved a tearful goodbye, watching Frank as he strode with his kitbag down the street and out of sight. His ship was sailing the next day and she would not be seeing him till... the next time, whenever that would be.

Next morning a letter arrived bringing news of her father's death. She was saddened because she had imagined that one day she would receive his forgiveness. He had never seen his grandchild and now it was too late. Unable to travel up to the village for the funeral at that stage in her pregnancy, she was still grieving her loss when she gave birth to Anna, six weeks later. Four days after that Frank was torpedoed. His ship went down with all hands. Quite devastated and for more than a year lost and uncertain about what to do, she eventually decided to seek peace and a place for the children away from the bombs and devastation of London. Now her father was dead she felt a growing need to be near her mother.

With almost as much trepidation as she had left Cwm Wylfa, Lydia returned. This time better dressed, a mature woman with two children of her own. She all but failed to recognise the woman who opened the door. Pitifully thin, hair almost white, her mother reached out a little unsure.

"Lydia?" It was an emotional return and the tears flowed freely, but they were tears of happiness, of relief that at last they were reunited. Her mother had lost none of the warmth that she had always shown and it wasn't long before she captured the hearts of her new-found grandchildren. Not only did they become acquainted with their nain, but she provided boiled eggs and bread with real butter for their tea, a luxury they hadn't known in London.

Lydia sighed as she looked through the window of the bus and out over the bracken covered slopes which her children had grown to love. This place had been in their blood she thought as she recalled the way they had taken to living in the village. And now they were grown up with families of their own. Ralph travelling the world, conducting and composing; how proud his father would have been. Anna was living nearby in Caernarfon, a qualified teacher, back at work after bringing up her own family.

Eliza never married. Ivor and she had drifted in and out of each other's lives for the remaining years of the war and then quite suddenly he had married a woman pregnant from a liaison with a G.I. and settled on the south coast somewhere.

"Mad as a hatter, always was," had been Eliza's pronouncement on hearing the news, and a few weeks later, demobbed from the A.T.S. she too had returned to Cwm Wylfa, accepted by one and all as if she had never been away. Her presence had helped Lydia and here they were as thick as ever, in spite, or could it be because of all the years between?

Lydia had to admit that she sometimes felt rather intimidated in her friend's presence. Eliza's independence together with her years in the A.T.S. had given her an enormous self confidence which at times led to embarrassing and undesirable confrontations with total strangers. She appeared to get a certain satisfaction out of these occasions, almost as though she was back in her position of sergeant major and addressing the ranks. Any time it happened, Lydia found it easier to fade into the background assuming anonymity with the inevitable audience.

Eliza materialised hugely at the bus stop outside the chapel. She stood in all her rotund majesty, corsetted and cosseted against the inclement weather. She stood so close to the step that young Robbie, about to dismount felt it necessary to be polite.

"S'cuse me please," he ventured when Eliza showed no apparent hurry to move aside and allow him to get off.

"Patience young man," she replied, standing her ground and making it impossible for young Robbie and his school friends to get off. They stood patiently waiting while she folded her umbrella, pocketed her gloves and took out her purse. There were other people waiting at the stop with expressions of resignation on their faces. Eliza was well known and tolerated in the village, but occasionally, as now, a stranger's patience was tested a bit too far.

5. DAN JONES

A tiny mouse of a man, raincoat collar turned up and flat cap pulled low dared,

"Urry up woman, we 'avn't got all day." He stood on tip-toe and winking at Dave through the window feigned a pushing movement behind the ample buttocks. Eliza chose this moment to step back and allow Robbie to exit. The flat cap and raincoat disappeared and became a stifled yell from the pavement. The school children collapsed in giggles.

The drama of the occasion was too good for Eliza to allow it to pass. She began to accost the red faced mouse who was picking himself up. One or two other people took the altercation as an excuse and pushing past the combatants, entered the bus.

"Hurry up please," shouted Dave, afraid that the argument would further hold up his schedule. He need not have worried however, for the mouse was more of a man than he appeared. Pushing past Eliza and thrusting a fistful of coins in Dave's direction, he snorted,

"Shut up woman, 'twas your stupid fault. 'Tis me should be complainin' not you." However, it was only a blunt pin with which he pricked the balloon of Eliza's pride. Undeflated, she paid her fare and undulated down the bus to join her friend whilst loudly condemning the stupidity of other people.

Dave winked into the driving mirror where he saw reflected, the face of the man who had taken the seat vacated by Robbie. The face smiled back. It spoke,

"You don't remember me do you? Dan Jones... Llangorse. Your Dad and mine were second cousins or something. We met once when we were kids... at Auntie Mary's. Remember?"

"Good heavens man that's years ago now. What brings you to these parts?"

"Brought the grandchildren back last night. My son lives in one of them rebuilt cottages, down Cwmbran. His wife's just 'ad 'er third. Another boy it was. By heck the other two led us a bit of a dance I can tell you. Full of energy. My wife were glad they wasn't stayin' no longer."

Dave laughed. "That time at Auntie Mary's we were in trouble most of the time I seem to remember."

"Aye, she didn't appreciate having her hen house burned down," they laughed, recalling the day and all that led up to their act of sabotage.

6. SABOTAGE

It was Auntie Mary's eightieth birthday. She was one of those vaguely related members of the family whose connection was never clearly understood by any of them. The children from three branches of the family found themselves together one day at her house. Their parents sat indoors talking and sipping endless cups of tea. The children were bidden to remain outside, supplied with a jug of lemonade, some biscuits and strict instructions not to get dirty.

Dave was there with his one sister and Dan with his two. There were three other girls, cousins apparently, but previously unknown to the boys. Dan quizzed them as to their ages and where they lived. Satisfied, he announced that all the girls could play together while he and Dave went off and did more important things.

"I'm not stayin' with that soft lot," he announced. "All they think about is playin' house and puttin' dolls to bed an' stuff." Dave agreed.

"What shall we do then?" They stood surveying the overgrown garden. Knee high grass bordered a path which led uphill away from the cottage and over the brow of the hill. The two boys turned automatically in this direction, Dave glancing back to make sure that his sister wasn't following. She had an awful habit of clinging on to him when they were somewhere strange. Today though, she was showing none of her usual signs of shyness having immediately joined with the other girls to play house. They were busy organising chairs and Dan's eldest sister was announcing with authority that she would be mam.

The boys reached the end of the path and found a padlocked gate, beyond which a meadow sloped away, out of sight of Auntie Mary's cottage. A rickety looking wooden hen house sat plumb in the centre of the field. Several strands of rusty barbed wire wound round rotten wooden posts separated the boys from this paradise. It took only seconds to find the weakest point at which to cross and to start down the slope. Dave barely noticed the green stains on his best grey socks, or the hole in his Sunday trousers where the wire had snagged.

They explored the hen house but there were few hens in residence, most of them were scratching around outside. Dan found one broody hen, threw her out and began playing with the china egg he found beneath her. He sat on one of the perches which promptly snapped under his weight, impressing on his trouser seat a pattern from white droppings. He peeped through the door, and having ascertained that the coast was clear, fished around in his pockets. Nonchalantly he offered Dave a cigarette.

"Hey, where d'you get these?" Dave was impressed.

"Easy. We've got a shop. I pinch 'em off the counter." He held a lighted match towards Dave.

"Here quick or I'll drop it." Dave fumbled the cigarette into his mouth and put the other end to the flame. He breathed in and spluttered out. Choking and gasping for the next few minutes he didn't see Dan light up and sit back like a veteran smoker. He didn't see the smug look on Dan's face either.

"Don't tell me that's your first time," smirked Dan when Dave's coughing had subsided. Dave shrugged,

"We haven't got a shop and me Mam and Dad don't smoke."

"Here, let me show you how to do it then," said Dan relenting. He put the cigarette between his lips and drew his mouth into a tight lipped smile while taking a deep breath. His eyes rolled inwards to the bridge of his nose and his eyelids fluttered. Momentarily Dave felt a shock of fright as he watched the other's grimace. Then Dan's shoulders relaxed and his eyes returned to normal as he breathed out a cloud of smoke. Running feet heralded the arrival of one of the girls. It was Dan's eldest sister.

"You've got to come back to the garden, you aren't allowed here." Her eyes suddenly took in the smoke and the packet of cigarettes. "Dan Owen, I'm going to tell. You've been pinching cigarettes again."

"Tell tale. That's all you think about, runnin' to mam with tales."

"Well... give me your chapel money and I'll keep quiet."

"Alright, if you promise." Dan suitably chastened stood up, stuffed the cigarettes and matches in his pocket and pronounced that he supposed they had better go. They returned the way they had come, but in far less immaculate condition.

"Our mam'll have your hide when she sees you," Dan's sister said with glee. "You should see your backside." She went off into peals of laughter and giggling, pointed out the source of her amusement to the other girls. It was at this moment that their mother came out of the house to ask if they wanted any more lemonade. She took one look at Dan and her face shrivelled.

"You little devil," she squeaked. "I told you to keep those clothes clean. A fine sight you'll look in chapel this evening. Your father had better deal with this." She caught hold of his sister, "Nia, go and fetch your Dad." Her voice was calm now, but there was something ominous about it. Dave stood rooted to the spot, aware now of the less than spotless clothes that he himself wore. He polished the toe of his shoe on the back of his other leg. With horror, he found the tear in his trousers. He was trying to replace the flap of material when his mother appeared and the smile died on her face.

The rest of that afternoon was sheer misery. The two boys were made to strip down to their underpants and have a good wash and the water, drawn directly from the pump in the yard, was icy cold. Their trousers were hung above the kitchen range after their mothers sponged them clean. They were ordered to clean their dirty shoes with rags and polish after which they had to sit in their underpants and shirts in the tiny kitchen, while the living room door stood open in order that they could be observed. Auntie Mary never said a word, but eyed them with disdain. She looked like the picture of Queen Victoria on the class-room wall.

Dan's father, confronted by the cigarettes discovered in the pocket of his trousers, promised him a thrashing the next day. He couldn't deal out such punishment on 'the Sabbath'. That nicety however was forgotten in the heat of the moment when a plume of smoke announced the immediate demise of the hen-house. Both boys spent an uncomfortable hour and a half on the hard chapel pews that evening.

Dan chuckled, recalling the many times he had thought about that day.

"I wonder how it 'appened? I thought about it a lot, but I never remembered what I did with that cigarette after Nia burst in on us." Dave grunted, he still couldn't admit to a long held guilt, a guilt which had afforded him nightmares for months afterwards. He could still picture the narrow ledge, where he had deposited that evil tasting cigarette; could still see the red line around the paper and the snake of ash on the dry, rotten wood.

"Doesn't matter much now," he replied. "I just hope we didn't incinerate any odd hen that strayed back into the place."

"The only thing they found in the ash was a china egg." Dan laughed. "Even in all that heat it never hatched." He laughed again, "but I saved my chapel money."

"I didn't understand about that," Dave said.

"Oh just a wheeze we 'ad for getting a bit of pocket money. Nia and me couldn't sit in the same pew as mam, dad and Anwen, we 'ad to sit in the pew in front. They gave us each a three penny bit for the collection. One day before chapel, I swapped mine for three pennies and put one in the collection and kept two. Next week I did the same but Nia noticed. My Dad never caught on and it meant that I 'ad a bit of private cash, but Nia soon learned to use it as blackmail."

"We moan about the youngsters now," Dave said. "Strikes me some of us were just as bad. The only difference today... their consciences don't bother them afterwards."

7. GRACE JONES

He was so lost in thought for a few minutes that he all but missed Grace Jones' house. He pulled up at the little gate beside the "B and B" sign and was about to toot the horn when she stood up behind the dense hedge. Wispy grey hair tumbled around a rosy, brown face which was all that could be seen of her.

"Bore da, Dave. Just pulling a few weeds..... Jim phoned to say you had some parcels." Dave exited the cab, reached inside and lifted out the two boxes of paperbacks...

"Pop them in the porch for me, there's kind of you." He hurried to the front of the house leaving the engine of the bus ticking over quietly. She smiled as he returned.

"I'm coming with you... popping in to see Angharad," she added, clambering up the steps, breathing heavily. Dave shut the door and returned to his seat. He had better get a move on or he would be running late.

The bus was on the last half mile before the main Bangor to Caernarfon road. He could see the halt sign coming up. At that moment an ambulance turned in towards Cwm Wylfa, sirens blaring, it passed swiftly on its way.

Looking in the rear-view mirror, Dave noticed all heads turned to watch as the ambulance hurried on its way. Everyone was anxious at the sight of such a vehicle, but possibly it was most poignant for Albert.

8. ALBERT

Among his friends, Albert was considered to be quite a celebrity. They none of them knew anyone else who had earned three medals. He earned his first medal during world war two, the second at the scene of an air crash and the third at the National Eisteddfod. He didn't look like a celebrity if one expects a celebrity to have something different about them, some kind of dynamism. Albert looked quite ordinary. He was muscular, but slightly built with a pleasant, open, wind weathered face and greying, thin hair. His expression was that of a happy, contented man and the crinkles round his eyes showed a talent for laughter.

Had anyone asked Albert which medal made him proudest, he would have unhesitatingly answered his last. He had a theory. Acts of so called bravery in the face of grave personal danger were, on his part anyway, simple reflex actions. He knew that on neither of the first two occasions had he weighed up the possible consequences of his actions, but simply found his feet taking him there. Some people were shocked into being routed to the spot. That didn't brand them cowards so why should he be branded a hero? To Albert, it was all a matter of reflexes.

When the C.O. and his mate were caught in the shell blast, they were injured and he was not. What else would anyone do but try and help? The fact that there was a munitions store behind their position was beside the point. The shells could kill him easily without any extra help that might give. He had dragged the men to the safety of a ditch with that in mind.

In retrospect he had undoubtedly been lucky. The shells were whistling past at a rate of knots and none of them hit him, or set off the ammunition until he was well clear. At the time the medal was presented, he hadn't thought about the question of bravery. He simply experienced, a vague sense of uneasiness at accepting it.

Years later when the war was just a distant memory, the air crash happened. He was helping his brother to round up the sheep on the slopes above Llyn Ogwen. They had stopped to watch as some fighter aircraft screamed up the valley at an unbelievable speed. His brother had walked on with the dogs, calling back,

"One day 'Bert there'll be an accident, you mark my words." Ten minutes later, two young pilots proved him right.

The fighter-jets had flown up the valley, peeled off to either side and disappeared from view for five or more minutes before repeating the exercise. He didn't know what happened, it was all too quick. One minute they were heading towards him and the next there was an explosive sound and wreckage was spinning to earth.

The bulk of one plane dropped on to the road at the end of the lake. Two cars travelling from Betws-y-Coed were lost to sight behind the smoke and flames which shot up after the impact.

The other plane landed in the lake, spouts of water leaping into the air as pieces of metal hit the surface. Then, in comparative slow-motion came a figure, hanging puppet-like below a parachute. The pilot landed like a stone while his parachute floated down and spread itself over him. There was no sign of movement under the silky shroud, but from the outline it appeared that the pilot's head was still above water.

Albert knew little about planes, but he did know that there were such things as ejector seats. He figured that somehow, although the pilot had been thrown clear of the plane, he was no longer conscious. He might be dead, but there was a chance... As the thought occurred to him, Albert found his feet running towards the lake. He wasn't a good swimmer, the water was icy cold, deep but at least calm. He waded out until his foot found nothing beneath and he was swimming with an urgency that excluded all else from his mind. He pulled the parachute towards him as soon as he reached it, uncovering a head and shoulder.

Mercifully, the pilot was in some kind of life jacket, but it didn't appear to be properly inflated. He was at a peculiar angle, with his face a few inches above the water. Albert anxious to stay clear of the parachute which threatened to wrap itself around him, grasped a handful of the silk, turned and headed for the shore. It was a journey that seemed endless. The weight he was pulling grew more by the minute and it was all he could do to move a few inches at a time. As if in a sea of treacle, he swam slowly, painfully, numb from the cold, while his brother who couldn't swim at all, called to him anxiously from the bank.

Motorists held up by the events, produced blankets, first aid boxes and thermos flasks with warm tea. They did what they could for the pilot, wrapping him in coats and rugs when they realised he was still alive, and helped fellow motorists who had been caught in the maelstrom of flying debris from the crashed plane. Everyone waited anxiously for help to arrive, assuming someone in the lakeside cafe would have reported the crash.

When Albert's exertions were over, his body reacted and he passed out, unaware of the ambulance arriving and the journey to hospital. Next day he read all about himself in the local and national papers. He also found out about the poor young pilots. The one whom he had saved was alive. Stunned when he was ejected, he now lay in intensive care with back injuries and a broken leg. The second pilot had not survived but the people in the cars had by some miracle, suffered only minor injuries. A matter of twenty seconds earlier and the plane would have landed on top of them. Following a second day under observation, Albert was discharged from the hospital. Local people petitioned his M.P. and wheels started turning. The following year he was in London again for a second medal presentation.

The medal that he won at the Eisteddfod was different. It really had to be earned and that involved a measure of hard work. Albert had always been an enthusiastic choir member but he was very surprised when Mr. Davies, the choirmaster, suggested that he sing the tenor solo in The Messiah.

"Oh, I don't know about that," he had replied somewhat startled at the idea. "There's plenty better voices than mine."

"Not in my choir there aren't, now you think on," Mr. Davies had insisted. Albert had decided to accept the challenge.

He had been thirty four and recently demobbed from the army when he first sang that solo. Rather nervous about the whole thing, he had gone along to Mr. Davies' home two or three nights a week to receive instruction. He learned how to breathe, to produce the best tone and most necessary of all, to overcome nervousness. Strangely, on the first night that they had performed "The Messiah," he had concentrated so much on doing justice to the music that he had forgotten to be nervous at all. Uplifted, was the only way he could describe his feelings, and he had thrown his soul into the part.

The local paper had praised him highly. He couldn't believe that they were referring to him. They talked about,

'This previously undiscovered talent', and 'The golden voice'. One local critic, ex-lecturer in music at the University told how he had enjoyed the 'meliffluosity' of this new tenor. Albert had failed to find the word in his dictionary. Spurred on by the favourable comments, he had never refused solo parts after that.

Out on the hillsides with the sheep he would practise, producing his dulcet tones to an unappreciative audience. Bryn, his dog, wasn't exactly keen either. Whenever Albert let rip, Bryn would slink along, ears flat, looking decidedly dejected. Odd invitations began to arrive with the post. Would he kindly consider singing at a party to be arranged for the over sixties? Sing at the wedding of Ceryl to Emlyn? Sing on the occasion of the Bishop's Cathedral Restoration Fund Thanksgiving? All these he gladly accepted, singing his heart out with endless pleasure and enjoyment.

He continued to take advice from singing experts after the death of Mr. Davies, finally going to Don Price, an ex-professional, now retired in Rhos. Don was a character who not infrequently told Albert that he was too old, that his voice was "bloody awful" but who in the next breath shouted praise.

"Damn good that was. Pity I didn't get you years ago. Could have done something with you then. Now what about the National Eisteddfod?" And so Albert entered the competition and won the first prize in the tenor section. He entered and won in the next four local Eisteddfods and the next year's National. On the sixth occasion he felt inclined just to go and enjoy listening to others. He never took part again, but he went to the National festival every year and he continued to accept invitations to sing in private gatherings as before.

At one Eisteddfod years later, when Albert was fifty eight, Lord Peris stepped on to the rostrum to announce that he was to award a special medal each year to the person in Wales, deemed to have done most to lighten the lives of everybody, but especially the old and sick in the community.

"In view of all the work he has done, singing in the hospital wards, to people in pensioner's homes, at meetings and clubs throughout the area... at his own expense in time and travel... I should like to award this, the first medal, to our friend here. Albert, would you step forward?"

Albert was noticeably slowing down now and the travel that his engagements entailed was making him tired. Visits he had made over the years to various venues had taken a toll of his energy and he couldn't roam the hillsides any more without twinges of rheumatism. Albert had accepted the medal knowing that this time his conscience could rest easy.

As he sat on the bus, his mind wandered to thoughts of his job. Happistores was a good name, because he was happy there. Nearly every day he would chat with someone who remembered him singing. He didn't live in the past, but it was nice to have regular proof that he had really earned that last medal.

Outside the rain clouds were breaking up, but people were still pulling coats and scarves tight against the cold wind. Behind him Albert could hear Eliza Jones's voice and that of her more subdued friend Lydia as they chatted. A motorbike passed the bus at some speed and Albert briefly saw the enormous beast. It was one of those shiny black Japanese machines with a rider who looked as black and shiny in his leathers and helmet as the bike itself. It was gone in a jiffy and Albert resumed his survey of the passengers. He looked across the aisle at young Moira who was unusually quiet and didn't look very cheerful, he thought.

9. MOIRA

She was lost in her own thoughts and they were not happy. Her usually bright and attractive face bore a worried expression and intermittently she returned to her childhood habit of nail biting. Her mother's words were still ringing in her ears.

"Don't come crying to me, you got yourself into this mess. Just remember, truth will out." The hackneyed cliche struck home this time. "No good sitting there, crying. You know the rights and wrongs of the matter. You must do what you know to be right."

But what should she do? Would it be any use explaining to the manager why she had to leave only a matter of weeks after starting work there? She curled up in dread at the very thought. The man intimidated her at the best of times so how could she tell him? Yet in her heart she knew that she must. He mustn't hear about it from someone else. Oh, how could she have been so irresponsible?

It had all started the previous Friday at lunch time. Because Sandra was celebrating her birthday, the younger members of staff had gathered in the Castle Bar. Moira felt a bit out of place, never having been to a bar before. She knew she was naive compared with most other girls of eighteen because her strict non-conformist parents had not allowed her the freedom her peers enjoyed. Unused to drinking and not knowing what to ask for, she had said she would have the same as Sandra.

Sandra's choice was a vodka-tonic and it would have been alright if Moira had stuck to that, but she found it tasteless and rather disappointing.

Alcohol, 'the demon drink' as her parents referred to it, obviously wasn't all it was cracked up to be. If she was going to enter this new adult world, she might at least enjoy it. When Peter suggested another round she let him buy her a martini instead. At least that had some taste and her initial curiosity had been satisfied, but then another martini appeared in front of her, someone else had bought a round. She didn't like to be rude, so she drank it, hoping no one would buy any more, because by now she was beginning to feel distinctly odd.

The conversation around her was lively, but she couldn't concentrate. She had an overwhelming urge to go to sleep. Making an effort she tuned in to a conversation about security procedures. They seemed to be talking about thieves and bank robberies, finger-prints and video cameras. Someone said,

"Statistics show that most robberies are carried out with inside help. Awful to think you could be working alongside a potential informant." They all stopped for a moment and eyed each other. Sandra broke the silence with an uneasy laugh.

"Not a nice thought on my birthday, here let's have a toast to honesty." They all raised their glasses and relaxed again.

"But you never really know how good security is till it's tested," Peter said. "Perhaps one of us should pretend to steal something and see if we can get away with it."

"How d'you mean?" Simon wanted to know.

"Well... supposing, for instance, I stole something... everyone knowing I'm going to do it, of course... but not what I'm going to take, or when. Not cash, but something confidential perhaps."

"Sounds a bit dicey," Simon commented, then glancing at his watch,

"Hey folks, time we were back at our posts."

Moira felt rather light-headed for the rest of the day, but believed that her lunch-time experience proved she had really grown up. She was the most junior member of staff and as such did all kinds of odd jobs from simple filing to carrying messages. That afternoon she went about in a ridiculously happy and relaxed state. When Peter asked her to put a large envelope in his brief-case, she was eager to please and did so without question.

Yesterday morning she arrived at the bank to find Simon and Peter in the middle of a furious row. Simon protested,

"How could you be such an imbecile?"

"I was only trying to prove a point," Peter argued, but Simon, his face registering his rage stalked out through the door. Moira asked one of the girls what it was all about.

"Apparently Peter put some papers in Simon's briefcase yesterday and Simon took them home, quite innocently. He found them late last night with that note." She indicated a slip of paper lying on the desk. Moira read,

JUST TESTING SECURITY AS PROMISED.

"Simon is absolutely furious. It was confidential stuff which shouldn't leave the bank."

"What did the manager say?" Moira felt shaky.

"Oh it hasn't reached his holiness's ears. Peter's put the papers back now, so I suppose it needn't go any further."

Mindful of the envelope which she had handled the previous day, Moira knew instinctively that it had contained the papers in question, so it meant that she was implicated. When Peter had pointed to the briefcase she had believed that it was his own. She didn't even question what he asked her to do, but she realised now that without those strange drinks inside her, she would have done. Going against all that she had been brought up to believe, kidding herself that she was a sophisticated adult, she had betrayed the trust the bank had put in her.

Her mind turned the matter over and over all day. She couldn't decide what to do although she kept coming back to the fact that honesty was always the best policy. But if Mr. Thomas the manager was unaware of the whole episode, was it really up to her to tell him? Must she tell him or could she 'let sleeping dogs lie'? Conscience stricken and sick with worry, she'd had a sleepless night.

She had poured out the whole sorry story at breakfast this morning, receiving like a physical blow, her mother's scandalised outburst. She dreaded even more having to go back home at the end of the day to face her father's wrath as well. How could she ever explain leaving her job? There really was no option but to go to the manager and admit to her part in the silly game Peter had played. Mr. Thomas was bound to find out about it sooner or later and she preferred to admit her stupidity now, before someone else told him. She must find the courage to apologise, and then she would leave with what dignity she could, and go straight to the job centre.

She squirmed on her seat, her heart thumping so strongly that in glancing down she half expected it to be obvious through her clothing. Then again, wrapped up in her thoughts, she sat tense and unaware of her surroundings. Over and over in her mind she enacted the scene that was to come in the manager's office.

10. DAVE REMEMBERS

Dave became aware that the passengers had suddenly fallen quiet. The bonhomie of the first part of the journey had given way to a pensive silence. Glancing in his rear-view mirror he could see that Moira was staring into space, apparently seeing nothing, Grace and Albert were looking out of the windows. Eliza was quiet too, but she appeared to have lost something about her ample bosom for she was plunging her strong, manly hand inside the neckline of her dress and squirming around on the seat.

Poor Lydia, embarrassed as ever, was squashed between her friend and the window. Suddenly with a shrill of triumph, Eliza withdrew her hand and held aloft a large safety pin. Then contorting herself she pulled her dress off one shoulder and attempted to replace the pin amongst a forest of shoulder straps.

Dave drew up at the halt sign and waited for the passing traffic before turning out on to the main Bangor road. He passed the new sign for Troed-y-Rhiw, all freshly painted, its coat of arms picked out in gold, glistening in spite of the dull day. In the distance, beyond the wall which encircled the Peris estate and at this point bordered the road, he could see a few passengers waiting at the stop outside the new comprehensive school. It wasn't yet completed, but hundreds of local people claimed this ultra modern glass and metal structure was out of keeping with the area. A battle of words had taken place in the council chambers and the press for over three years, but the need for a new, larger school, offering facilities beyond most people's imaginings would not go away. It seemed nothing could be done to halt the relentless march of both modernity and necessity.

Dave stopped and as the passengers entered the bus, he dispensed tickets or checked season tickets as required. Pulling away from the stop he saw the level crossing gates were in his favour and was glad there was no sign of the unhelpful Jane Evans who manned them. Bumping over the railway lines he could see ahead to the group of people waiting at the Golden Fleece. The old stone building was graced by a beautifully executed sign hanging above the door. This, like the village sign had been recently painted, but unlike its neighbour glistened in the sunshine which was now appearing sporadically. Dave thought the weather was definitely turning out better than he had expected and his mind turned to his little garden and the weeding he needed to do.

In Troed-y-Rhiw as in most of the villages around, there were two schools of thought where pubs were concerned. According to whichever you belonged, the Golden Fleece was thought of as The Lost Sheep, or as Paradise. Therefore when a passenger on alighting called to his friend,

"See you in Paradise," he wasn't referring to his final departure. That, according to his wife, would see him in a very different place.

Dave remembered passing the Golden Fleece one Saturday night in early December. Bangor had won the match that day in spite of all expectations to the contrary. The Troed-y-Rhiw fans needed no better excuse to celebrate and were doing so noisily. Dave's final trip took him past the pub just on closing time. He was relieved he had no passengers at that point because to his consternation, a group of fans decided to climb on board, in spite of the fact that most of them lived within half a mile or so. Having spent all their money on beer, they could not afford the small fare to Bangor where they decided, one and all, they must go. Dave couldn't move them single handed and didn't want to risk a scene. He decided to carry on to Bangor and hope they would have the sense to get off quietly. He knew most of the men by sight and could rejoice with them, the fact that Bangor had won. He moved off down the hill and out of the village.

Just half a mile on was a lay-by and on impulse Dave pulled in and stopped.

"All out," he shouted, but no one intended leaving. "Come on now, you'd all be best at home. You don't want to go to Bangor at this time of night." This was met with a chorus of whistles and protestations.

"Get a move on," someone shouted. Again Dave attempted to persuade his unwelcome passengers to get off the bus, but they refused.

"We want to go to Bangor." Irwin's dimple chinned face slid into view over the back of a seat. "D'y hear me?" He asked wagging a finger at Dave.

"An' if you don't take us... I'll come up there and teach you a lesson, Dave Owen," he added, throwing his fist in the air. As his friends shouted encouragement, Irwin's eyes met on the bridge of his nose and slowly he disappeared from sight behind a seat. Dave seeing no way out of this predicament, was about to close the hydraulic doors and get going when there was a piercing whistle and a yell,

"Bryn, come on boy," and with this a collie suddenly bounded up the steps and in to the bus. Bright eyed, tail wagging and panting hard, he made his way down the bus till he located his master, barked once and waited expectantly. He was mildly diverted, finding he was sharing the floor of the bus with various animals of the human species, so he went from one to another, sniffing them and licking their sweaty faces. Great hilarity greeted his arrival and much fuss was made of a dog which in the sober daylight would be treated as the lowliest of servants.

Two male passengers waiting at stops before Bangor were quick to appraise the situation as they boarded, so they stayed quietly at the front of the bus with Dave.

"What you goin' to do with that lot?" one enquired, jerking his thumb.

"I don't rightly know," Dave admitted, "I'm just hoping they'll get off quiet like." Five minutes later he passed the castle and breathed a sigh of relief; not long now. He had stopped for one of his recent passengers to alight when a voice shouted,

"He's a traitor... where's his colours?" There were shouts and jeers as the man scuttled away into the darkness and the remaining individual hid from sight on the steps of the bus.

At the depot, Dave pulled into the cleaning area and suggested his innocent passenger make a quick getaway. Gratefully he took his chance, but he was not quick enough and with a cry the pack were after him. Dave saw him disappear through the entrance to the pedestrian bridge and sighed with relief when the others didn't notice.

Thinking of his own escape, he turned off the lights, locked the bus and melted into the shadows. He made his way to the office and left the keys with the security man. Collecting his Mini from the staff car park, he nosed it out into a deserted street.

He never quite knew what happened to the Bangor supporters that night. They hit the local headlines and some of them ended up in cells till morning. They were fined heavily by the court for drunk and disorderly behaviour and visits to Paradise had to be postponed till their wives had forgiven them and they had earned enough cash to drink once more.

Dave brought his thoughts back to the present as he saw, huddled in the shelter of the Golden Fleece doorway, two old men who were occasional passengers. They stood together like poor characters in a Victorian novel, looking cold and malnourished. Herb, leaning on his stick, was a kindly old man, his pale eyes and bushy beard making him look much like the popular idea of an absent minded professor. Beside him stood Dafydd, the 'Mr. McGoo of Troed-y-Rhiw', his sparse, lanky frame and jerky movements reminiscent of a puppet. Dark framed, round lenses sat on the end of his nose and he lifted his chin when speaking to his friend in order to see through them.

A little apart, stiff and arrogant in bearing was a young man whom Dave recognised as Emlyn Acre. An odd one that fellow, something almost weird about him, Dave thought, not for the first time. He wondered why Emlyn was travelling by bus and not in his own car. Such was the man's reputation however, that Dave was not inclined to bother asking, or even to pass the time of day.

Two giggling teenagers, shop assistants in Woolworths, ran out from the ladies toilet at the side of the pub. They hurried past the men and were first to board the bus. They were an exasperating pair, always shedding scarves or bags or dropping coins when they were about to pay their fare. They must keep lost property departments in business, Dave thought ironically as they made their way down the aisle, thoughtlessly shedding sweet papers. The two old men greeted Dave with smiles, laughing at their inability to get up the steps easily. They took their time while Emlyn glowered behind them. Dave dealt with their tickets, closed the door and engaged the gears.

11. EMLYN'S PROBLEM

Emlyn moved down the bus in the wake of the two older men. He looked smart in his modern, well cut clothes. His suit, though dark, was not redolent of the last family funeral, as was that of some men he knew. His tie was what the most fastidious valet might call quiet and his shoes showed no sign of wear. He clutched a black and chrome fibreglass brief-case with combination locks which, after selecting a seat, he placed beside him like the arm of a chair.

It wasn't far to the next stop and already the bus was slowing down. Seeing who was waiting, Emlyn consciously moved his brief-case so that it occupied most of the seat beside him. There was no way he intended to share the empty seat with anyone; because he didn't feel like talking to people he didn't know. He wasn't a very sociable person and over the years people had got used to his quiet way. They just nodded when they saw him and rarely initiated conversation, but had any of his fellow travellers been able to read his mind on this occasion, they would have been quite horrified, for Emlyn's thoughts had turned to murder.

He watched the reflections in the window as Netta Jenkins heaved herself up and on to the bus. She was so enormous it was remarkable she managed it at all, he thought without the slightest compassion. If his mother looked like that, he would have got rid of her years ago. With relief he watched a gasping Netta Jenkins fall thankfully into the nearest seat at the top of the steps. Fancy having to share a seat with her, he shuddered.

With that, his thoughts returned to the problem of the moment. He was fed up with living under the same roof as his mother. He wanted an interesting life, something she had so far denied him. His ambitions were frustrated at every turn because she was always in the way. He found his routine monotonous in the extreme and there were many other disparaging adjectives he could think of to describe it.

The days always began the same, weekends or weekdays, it made little difference. He had to sit down to a `proper' breakfast and by that she meant bacon, egg and tomato, followed by toast and marmalade. He had always insisted on tea although he knew that she would much prefer him to have coffee. Not instant coffee, oh no. Nothing less than the real thing, percolated of course.

Sometimes it was all he could do to swallow what she put before him although it was always best quality and cooked beautifully. There was nothing over-greasy about it and the toast was always warm and crisp. He couldn't be better served in a five star hotel but even five star hotels could lose their attraction.

As long as he could remember, Emlyn had done as he was told. As a child he learned quickly that it paid off. On the few occasions he had transgressed, reaction had been swift and painful. His mother would stand between him and the door shouting,

"Go to your room. There will be no tea for you today." He would go, covering his head with his hands, but rarely avoiding the stinging slaps that reigned down as he squeezed past her. Later, drying his tears, he would sit on his bed feeling resentful, rebellious, scared and lonely in turn. He had loved his mother when she was nice, but she could be very hard if he broke the rules and it was then he came close to hating her.

He would be punished quite often for doing things that other parents accepted as normal for a young boy. He was not allowed to play in the street or to roam over the hills without an adult in charge. He never dared to go fishing or to collect tadpoles, for he knew his mother would not approve.

He was expected to play with his friends in the garden so she could keep an eye on them. This was something she insisted on, but it wasn't easy to play games on the narrow strip of grass she referred to as a lawn. If any of his friends came, the first thing they wanted to do was to climb the rock face alongside, but that wasn't allowed and nowhere was flat enough or a big enough area for football or cricket.

She had an awful habit of remonstrating with his friends when they did things he wasn't allowed to do. She would say in a superior voice,

"Now I'm sure you don't make a noise like that in your house."

Invariably the answer was a sheepish no, although Emlyn knew instinctively that they did. In their houses, making a noise was no crime.

He was made to invite his friends formally and had to be invited by them before any socialising was allowed, but Emlyn knew they all roamed in and out of each others' houses as the fancy took them. They couldn't appreciate that he wasn't allowed to do the same and began to look upon him as some kind of oddity. It wasn't long before they tired of his mother's rules and regulations and refused his invitations.

He knew what lay behind her paranoia of course. His mother had been in service on Lord Peris -Jones's estate. Originally a general help, she had later been assigned to assist the nanny, preparing meals for the children when cook was busy with family and guests. She also washed, ironed and mended for them and baby-sat when nanny was off duty. She learned how to set a table, use a napkin, all the ways in which children in the 'big house' were expected to behave. She observed the way the family conducted themselves, admired them and vowed to remember. It was her intention to rise above the common way of doing things and live graciously. She wouldn't ever be able to live as well, but she could do better than a lot in her walk of life.

She was courted by Bert Acre, clerical assistant to the manager of the estate. Bert had been to a grammar school and then trained as an office worker. She was flattered that he should be interested in her, an ordinary village girl. When he proposed marriage she didn't hesitate, visualising a rosy and secure future.

They set up home in a modernised gardener's cottage alongside the Bangor road at Troed-y-Rhiw, one of several leased to estate workers. With perks like provisions from the estate, a convenient bus to Bangor, and a small shop nearby, she lived a life of comparative ease. It was only blighted by their proximity to the Golden Fleece, but in spite of her initial reservations, even that wasn't a source of too much disquiet.

She turned the cottage into a little palace where everything was clean and shining. Emlyn's father started each day with a good breakfast inside him and had a good solid meal to come home to. He appreciated her attentions, but there were times when her insistence on observing the niceties of life got him down. He refused to wear Sunday best, arguing that as it was the day he relaxed, he preferred to be casual.

Bert never went to chapel. He was a content and relaxed agnostic so there was little point. She felt let down by his absence and particularly by his attitude. She couldn't even entertain anyone to Sunday tea, because Bert wouldn't dress suitably.

Emlyn loved his father and liked his independence of mind. He yearned to be the same, but his mother's dominance brooked no argument. An appeal to his father got him nowhere because preferring a tranquil atmosphere he would simply say,

"Do as your mother asks, there's a good boy. She means well, she's a good woman." Even though he guessed his father didn't always agree with his mother, Emlyn never heard him speak against her.

Wishing to please his father, Emlyn had done many things at his mother's behest which left him feeling humiliated or frustrated. How different she was from her neighbours who considered her too superior by far and most certainly 'not one of them'. Horrified, Emlyn realised one day that he had inadvertently adopted many of her ideas. He found himself judging his peers by the way they held their knife and fork, whether they carried a clean handkerchief or how well they spoke. This was not conducive to making friends of course for not everyone measured up to such expectations and he had to admit that indeed, he had few friends.

He had just begun his first term at the Comprehensive School when his father died. Emlyn grieved for him while at the same time sagging under the growing, oppressive domination of his mother. Now that Emlyn was all she had, she kept him around her constantly. The following years seemed like a series of,

"Yes mother, no mother, three bags full mother," and he was reaching the end of his tether. He attained the eight `o' levels she wanted. He had passed with good grades the three 'A' levels. He went to Bangor University and obtained a good degree in Physics. In all that time he had lived at home and behaved in the ways that she dictated.

As the bus drew level with Dolydd Garage, Emlyn peered through the showroom windows at the sleek, silver saloon he intended buying. Two more pay cheques and he would be able to put down over half the cost. He missed the convenience of the little runabout he had just sold. He'd got more for it in a private sale than the garage had offered in part exchange, so he had parted with it prematurely. Just wait till his mother saw that silver monster. He could visualize her face, proud and smug like his own, as they purred along the valley road past their neighbours.

But in fact it wasn't his mother's face he dreamed of seeing beside his own, but the bright little face of Sarah Hall. She worked in the same building and he often found himself alongside her in the lift, or the canteen. He felt excited every time he set eyes on her, often being rendered speechless. She always had a happy smile and he found her voice attractive. When he had that car he was going to ask her out. He would take her to dinner, at the wine-bar or The Castle, it had to be somewhere really top class. Going out to dinner meant leaving his mother for the evening and that required explanations, necessitated lies. He didn't want to subject Sarah to the inevitable inquisition, or he would end up being humiliated. The more he envisaged the scene the more convinced he became that he had to get rid of his mother, somehow. She wouldn't take a holiday or go anywhere without him. When he had suggested finding a place of his own she had thrown a fit of hysterics. He was thoroughly sick of the situation and had to do something or he would never be free.

Last night she went for a bath and he sat down to watch his favourite programme while he had peace and quiet. It didn't last. She was calling out, telling him to take out the bins, to make a cup of tea, anything it seemed, calculated to interrupt his television programme. He had cursed, wishing she would drown herself or something equally final. She would never conveniently drown in the bath, he knew, but he remembered a film where someone was killed when an electric heater fell into the water. Now that was a thought. Everyone knew water and electricity don't mix, but sometimes old ladies forget, grow careless, but not his mother. Still it was a possibility and he would have to think about it. He liked the idea. Surely an 'accident' shouldn't prove too difficult to arrange.

He got up from his seat and made his way towards the door behind Albert the parking attendant. The man was usually already in his kiosk when Emlyn passed in his car each morning. The car was so much more convenient he thought; using the bus meant getting up a whole hour earlier. It had been worth the effort though, to get a good price for his Fiesta.

Here on the outskirts of the town, fronting the main road, an enormous hangar-like building had appeared a few months back. It turned out to be a hypermarket smugly called Happistores, an ugly looking place surrounded by acres of car park which did nothing to enhance it. Dave slowed the bus and stopped. Albert saluted as he alighted and then with a light step walked towards the car-park entrance and the little wooden kiosk, his home for the day.

The throb of a powerful motor bike grew louder as it passed, giving out a strong smell of exhaust. The rider steered into the Happistores car park, stopping in the first space nearest to the road. He parked the heavy bike with ease and removing his crash helmet, revealed a close cropped head and a hard face. The nose had been broken at some time and a broad scar interrupted the jaw-line below one cheek. He had the solid muscular look of a boxer with powerful shoulders and a stocky body. His attitude was tense and alert like a wary animal.

Albert was reminded of men he knew in the army and of whom he had always been wary. By the time he had opened the kiosk door and was ready to issue a parking ticket the man had vanished. Well, Albert thought, he would be here when the man returned and he would certainly charge him if he had overstayed his allotted two hours.

Next door to the store was another new and very large square building. It resembled a glass box and it sat amid well manicured lawns. A green neon sign on the roof announced B & L Pharmacy and here Emlyn worked in a managerial capacity, having been promoted quite recently. He enjoyed his work and found the modern building an exciting environment. His attraction to Sarah Hall had added considerably to his pleasure lately and he anticipated seeing her again when he checked the progress of research in the lab. He tucked his brief case under his arm, walked up the tarmac drive between the green lawns and disappeared through the automatic glass doors.

12. THE JOINER

The skull like features and scrawny neck jerked forwards and raising his hand to his mouth Dafydd Parry indulged in a bout of coughing. He peered from watery eyes through the spectacles on the end of his nose as Albert made off towards his little wooden kiosk. It looked as if it could do with some attention, the cedar needing a coat of preservative and the shutter some repairs. Sitting back and pushing his glasses higher, he wondered if he could ask Albert to mention his name to the manager. Work would be welcome as he had nothing to do at the moment and he wanted to earn some money to add to his meagre pension. He studied his hands, which were the best part of him, still being strong and capable. They had done rough heavy work hewing trees, sawing and repairing wagons on the quarry railway. They were hands which also produced the most delicate work, lovingly planning and sanding, bringing out the character of wood, the beauty of the grain.

When the quarry closed, he discovered that there didn't seem to be any regular work for qualified joiners, so he took odd, short term contracts. He missed his little mini-van but could no longer afford to run it. It wasn't easy using the bus, because he often had to walk a long way beyond the bus-stop with his heavy tool-bag. Neighbours or people working in the same place would sometimes offer him a lift, but then the job would finish and he would have to start again somewhere else.

He had been employed by the hospital, the cinema, various hotels and the University. He had also worked on the new shopping centre and office blocks. He took pride in doing his best and was sorry that he had never had the opportunity to train as a master craftsman. All the things he made in his free time bore witness to his creative talent and craftsman's ability.

There were walking sticks with carved handles and wooden puzzles and toys. Some of his work had travelled far beyond Wales, bought by the bed and breakfast guests who once frequented their spare room. His carved cupboards and miniature bardic-chairs sold well to tourists at the local craft shop, but didn't bring in enough money for him and Bessie to live on. Severe arthritis prevented her from taking any more paying guests, so their combined finances had dwindled.

Sometimes it grieved him, the way life had changed. He felt that a certain appreciation and recognition of quality had disappeared to be replaced by the mediocre. Standards of behaviour and good manners were considered old fashioned nowadays and the Sabbath congregations were smaller than ever.

His childhood in the small village community had the chapel to guide and the quarry to provide. Everyone coped with the ups and downs of life helping each other along the way. Better education and new technology had much to answer for, because between them they had wrecked the safe world he loved. Yet he couldn't condemn progress; his children had done very well for themselves, he was just sorry they had needed to move away to do it. It was people like him and Bessie who watched as their world fell apart.

Life hadn't been easy: he was the fifth of nine children, some of whom never reached their teens. Born in the years of the depression, and growing up during world war two he never expected much from life, but he remembered in photographic clarity, all the happiest times. Colouring everything was the strong feeling of belonging, of being a part of it all.

He was only of average ability in school, but he always enjoyed his classes. At home on Sunday mornings, father lined up the family and held an inspection. They had to be certain their hands, faces and shoes were clean and clothes tidy because they couldn't afford special `Sunday best'. Afterwards father marched them down the lane, constantly reminding them not to scuff their shoes on the rough surface.

From chapel they would return home to the tasty lunch which mother prepared in their absence. They always made short work of the lamb and mint-sauce, roast potatoes and carrots, never noticing when she went without meat for their sake. They took it in turns to scrape the rice-pudding dish which was always a creamy delight, for they had plenty of milk, the local farmers saw to that.

After lunch they were put on their honour to go straight to Sunday school. Cissie the eldest was put in charge and they all knew better than to get on the wrong side of her. She was too ready, Sunday or not, with the flat of her hand and a flick of her wrist. They were home again for tea, then this time with mother, off to chapel once more.

When a boy's schooldays were over, he automatically looked to the quarry for work and Dafydd with his brother Tom and later Owen-John were no exception. While they learned the art of slate dressing, Dafydd was apprenticed to his uncle who was a joiner there. The daily requirements in the quarry were mainly in the field of repairs and maintenance, but in his spare time he enjoyed making things which showed off the beauty of the medium.

When he and Bessie were married, they rented Morwelfa cottage. They loved the place and it was still their home, but time and modern life passed them by, so now they often felt like flotsam on an outgoing tide.

Bessie had been a good wife and had borne him two sons and a daughter. They had tried to bring them up to be God fearing and respectable like themselves. He had to admit failure as far as the chapel was concerned because once the children reached their teens, they rebelled. At first he insisted on one visit to chapel each Sunday, but eventually he had given in to the children's' total disregard of the Sabbath as a day of God. Sadly, he realised, they were not alone among their peers..

He recalled one summer a few years back. The children had all left home and Bessie was still doing bed and breakfasts. He found work as and when he could and that year was lucky in obtaining several months of employment at the newly constructed quarry museum. After working in his usual capacity as joiner he stayed on as an attendant, explaining to tourists what all the machinery was for and how the quarry had functioned. Talking to a group of visiting clergymen about the locality, he learned that a little used church near the Menai Straits was being closed and sold.

"Terribly sad, terribly sad. Never thought I'd see the day," one of the dignitaries muttered.

Excitement registered on Dafydd's face. Important questions were forming inside his head making him agitated. He pushed his spectacles up on his nose. For years he had toyed with the idea of building an organ to give to his chapel. His friend Bob Tudor thought it would be a fun challenge to build an electronic one. Not knowing how to obtain keyboards, they had got no further than dreaming about the idea. But now, here might be the answer. Tentative enquiries elicited the fact that there was indeed an old, two manual organ about to be scrapped. A few phone calls later they spoke to the Vicar of the doomed church and he was able to grant them permission to remove it.

Enthusiastically they made the necessary arrangements, and went to the old church where they proceeded to dismantle it, carefully piece by piece. Bob was a farmer, fit and strong, and with arm muscles like a weightlifter. He had no trouble pulling apart the various parts of the organ, piling the best pieces together and tossing the broken bits in a bin. When it was full he carried it easily to his trailer outside and set to work again with renewed energy. He joked as they busied themselves, while Dafydd, trying to ignore his wheezing chest and the age difference between them struggled to keep up. He was thrilled to think his dream of many years was to see fruition. There was a lot of good mahogany with very little sign of woodworm and two keyboards, rather yellowed, but real ivory. Together they took all the unwanted bits and pieces to the tip, then returned to the church for the rest, loaded up and headed home. Back at Morwelfa cottage Bessie stood her ground in the doorway.

“I'm not having all that stuff in the house,” she said. “I know what it's like when you're just making simple toys; sawdust everywhere. I'm too old now to be cleaning up after you.” Dafydd tried arguing between coughs but Bessie was unmoved.

“Outside in the shed, or take it back where you got it from. You and your mad ideas. And you in the state you're in!”

He had been hurt. She spoke as though he was always doing crazy things. This was the first time he had got around to anything on such a scale, and he was banished... to the shed! Out there it would be cold, damp, draughty and without light. Did she think that might discourage him? Was that her way of stopping him? No, she couldn't be that cruel. She knew he was about to fulfill a long standing ambition, but how could they achieve anything out there?

He had reckoned without his partner who went home, returning later with cable and sockets, a roll of roofing felt and some off cuts of hardboard. He even had a piece of old stair carpet for the floor and a good light fitment.

“This stuff was all left over from when I built the room in the loft,” he smiled, “I thought it would come in useful one day.” An hour or so later, the shed had become a reasonable workplace. Once the cable was connected to the mains, there was no doubt that it would be a well lit area too. Bob needed different cable in order to connect to the mains indoors, so promised to get some from B & Q.

“I've got an old fan-heater somewhere,” Bob said. “I'll see if I can find that. Be useful later on.” By Easter the shed had become a good workroom.

Dafydd enjoyed pottering in his new 'den'. He spent hours studying his design and picking the best mahogany from the old organ to construct the new. In one big operation he laid out all the wood he intended using and treated it to kill any enterprising worm. Much time was taken discussing with his partner how all the electrical parts would fit. Bob cooperated happily and by the following spring they intended to have the organ completed.

Over Christmas Bob's time was taken up with family matters and then Dafydd had another bout of bronchial trouble in the January. Bessie refused to allow him to work in the shed for some weeks after he recovered, so it was well into spring before he could start work again.

The first shock was finding how much the damp had affected things. Rust and mildew had covered tools and woodwork and all the stops had swollen. It took him more than a week to bring everything back to prime condition. He rubbed down, stained, polished and only when he could once more slide his fingers smoothly along the grain patterns in the wood did he have the courage to phone Bob. Somehow they finished the project by the end of May. Bob hooked the trailer to his car and with two of his lads to help, they carefully transported the organ to the door of Capel Coch. Dafydd wanted to surprise the Minister, knowing he would be overjoyed with such a kind donation to the chapel.

But it was the Minister himself who delivered the surprise. He professed delight with the new organ and with the sentiments which led to its construction, but putting the tips of his fingers together, he frowned and assumed an air of commiseration.

"Due to the falling number in the congregation, I am instructed to Minister to four different chapels from June onwards. This chapel is of course one of them, but I'm afraid it means that I shall only be holding a service here once a month. If attendance numbers continue to decline it may even be necessary to close the chapel altogether and you will then be obliged to worship at Capel Peris. I am so sorry to be the bearer of such bad tidings... these modern times I'm afraid."

Bob was clearly disappointed but Dafydd was crestfallen. Subconsciously he had seen their organ as a beacon, an encouragement to come to chapel, to sing to the Glory of the Lord. Now it seemed there may not even be a chapel in which to sing at all. Capel Peris indeed! That wasn't his chapel, this was. Even as he protested he could see by the Minister's face that the battle was already lost.

"I'm afraid they already have a good organ in Capel Peris so I don't think they will need this one," the Minister said. "Of course, we 'll keep it here, indeed use it till such time as the chapel does close, for I am very much afraid it will, but we shall be pleased to use it till then. Perhaps afterwards we may be able to find it a home, you never know." His voice died away and he made a helpless movement with his arms. "I'm so sorry."

Subdued, they had moved the organ in to the chapel. The minister watched them as they struggled through the door, up the aisle and on to the low dais. Only now, newly enlightened as to the state of the real world, did Dafydd's eyes register the broken window pane, the stain on the floor from the leaking roof and the mildewed wall?

"God works in His mysterious way," the Minister intoned. "I wish I had better news for you, but rest assured your efforts will not have been in vain."

Wryly, Dafydd remembered the inauguration of the organ at the service on the following Sunday. Apart from Bessie, Bob and himself, there were only twelve people in the congregation. The occasion did not even merit a mention in the local paper. It was the wettest summer on record for twenty odd years and the chapel suffered badly from the damp. By autumn most of the stops on the organ had seized again. During the carol service at Christmas, the minister delivered the 'coup de gras'. The chapel would be closed from then on, due to lack of money for maintenance and the inability of such a small congregation to raise what was needed. In the New Year the building was advertised for 'Conversion to a Domestic Dwelling' and Bob retrieved the organ during one of Dafydd's spells in hospital. He had nowhere to put it, so it sat mouldering in the place where it was born, Dafydd's shed!

13. ANGHARAD

The bus was passing a row of terraced, stone cottages which stood back from the road behind a thick beech hedge. Five small gates interrupted its length and Dave, with a glance in his rear view mirror, drew to an unofficial stop at the fifth. He knew Grace Jones disliked the walk from the official stop further on, because there was no pavement. She made a quick exit from the bus, indicated her thanks, opened the gate bearing the legend 'Rush Pottery' and walked up to the house.

Fifteen minutes beforehand, Angharad Rush had picked up a pottery mug and hurled it at the stone wall.

"Damn, damn, damn," she watched as the mug shattered and fell in bits all over the slate floor. She pushed back the lock of black hair which kept falling over her face and hugged her arms to her body as a cold shiver ran through her. The slender figure and elegant legs exposed the beauty of the woman as she moved gracefully, to look out of the window.

It was seven years since she had embarked on her small business known as 'Rush Pottery'. She started out with enthusiasm, energy and all her savings, spending the first winter, working hard at her wheel. She had built up a large stock for the official opening at Easter and then spent the rest of the spring and summer selling that same stock to tourists eager to take home an attractive souvenir.

Her venture had been successful with few unsold articles, so she started optimistically on her second year with a fresh new colour scheme and brand new shapes. The second, third and fourth summers had gone well but come the fifth, there had been a definite drop in sales and a marked lack of interest. Last summer had been a complete washout literally and financially and here she was with the little shop still two thirds full.

She hadn't made anything new during the previous winter, lacking either money or energy to do so. Now she must face the fact that the pottery vogue had had its day, and so it seemed, had she.

"Oh Patrick," she cried, the emptiness since his death seeming never to lessen. "Patrick, why did you have to go? I begged you not to... oh my love." She threw herself into a chair and allowed herself to weep in a wave of self pity.

When they first met, she was a student on a working holiday in Llandudno. She had charge of a kiosk outside a big souvenir and gift shop. The blister-packs, toys and gaudy china had been moved out of the shop to be displayed on her counters. She was ashamed at first to ask money for some of the goods, considering them to be useless trash. Then she realised with amazement that she was selling to willing buyers. She couldn't imagine why anyone wanted to buy most of the stuff, but they undoubtedly did, so she lost her reserve and began actively promoting the sales. So successful was she that crowds began to collect, standing amused, listening to the friendly banter as she urged even more passersby to purchase souvenirs.

One evening she went to a little pub, popular with some locals, and a few particular tourists who, like the proprietor, disliked background music. There she fell into conversation with the bar attendant, a soft spoken Irish boy whom she guessed to be about the same age as herself. He had the most piercing blue eyes she had ever seen on anybody and with his tousled black hair framing an impish face, he was, she thought, quite attractive.

He was from Belfast, unsurprisingly called Patrick and like her, a student on a working holiday. His parents, anxious for him to get away from the province and earn his living in politically healthier climes, had suggested he applied to a college on the British mainland.

"I wanted to be reasonably near the ferry so I could get home easily," he explained. "So I ended up here in North Wales, teacher training college actually. I've got another year to do." "Didn't you want a holiday job nearer home?" she asked conversationally, but was unable to comprehend the expression which flickered over his face before he answered.

"Nothing doing in the way of work over there," he shrugged his shoulders, "not many tourists these days." He moved away to serve a customer.

She sipped her drink, gazing into space and not thinking of anything in particular. Suddenly, a picture formed in her mind. Patrick was floating gently in the air above brightly coloured flames which grew taller and taller, reaching up towards him. It was such a vivid picture that she shuddered, wondering why she should be cursed with second sight. Hastily she shut it out, screwing up her eyes and covering her face with her hands. She leaned forward to listen to what he was saying as he came back to her end of the bar. It was not a particularly busy night, so they enjoyed conversing, interrupted very occasionally by customers buying drinks. The more they chatted, the more Angharad was attracted to him and she found herself hoping that it was mutual.

"I've often watched you selling things." He smiled; unaware of the surge of emotion it created in the pit of her stomach.

"You've got a very persuasive way." He laughed, "I thought my people held the title... Irish blarney and all that." Angharad recognised in Patrick the embodiment of what he described, knew she was a willing victim. By the end of the week, the Irish magic had irretrievably cast its spell.

It soon became apparent that the attraction was not one sided and they attempted to see each other regularly. Their free time didn't often coincide, so she spent most evenings sitting in the bar where he worked. There was a knot of excitement in her stomach as she watched him exchange pleasantries with the customers. He had a face that looked as if it were chiselled into its masculine lines, firm square chin, wide laughing mouth, straight nose and broad forehead. Above this was the crown of black curly hair which tumbled casually over his ears and was a shade too long at the back. Sometimes in the morning before the bar opened, he would reverse the evening procedure and wander down to the kiosk to chat to her. By the end of the summer their relationship was becoming a serious matter.

They continued their courtship the following year, squeezing it in between their work at Bangor University. Angharad got her degree in History and Patrick; a dedicated and conscientious student obtained his teaching diploma. They celebrated by announcing their engagement. Patrick had not only fallen in love with a Welsh girl, but also with her country and Angharad soon had her fiancé well on the way to being fluent in her mother tongue.

Patrick was impatient to take her to Ireland. They went shortly before Christmas, but although his mother and father made her most welcome, nothing prepared Angharad for the scenes of desolation she found in the city. She could not shake off a feeling of oppression which made her feel guilty in the light of their hospitality. They were delighted with their prospective daughter in law and did all they could to show it. Gleefully, they took her on trips to meet relations in various villages nearby, but she was unable to rid herself of a sense of anxiety. Road blocks and soldiers with rifles did nothing to dispel the unease she felt the whole time she was there.

Her worries were thrust aside and forgotten when they married at Easter and settled in their tiny cottage. She had a job in Bangor University library and Patrick found a village school in Troed-y-Rhiw which was in need of a teacher. Working hard to repair and modernise their little cottage, they came home from work each day and turned themselves into plumbers, electricians and carpenters as the work demanded. There was a tiny guest room and Patrick's sister and current boy-friend came for a climbing holiday and used Rush Cottage as a base. Her in-law's too enjoyed many busy summer weeks helping with the garden and the cooking while she and Patrick were at work. At weekends there were picnics and sightseeing and Mrs. Rush enjoyed shopping trips in Llandudno. Three years went by, and then one evening they realized that their thoughts were continually returning to the subject of children.

"I know there were things we wanted before starting a family," Patrick said, "and I know we can't afford everything we'd like, but I feel quite jealous every time I see someone with a baby." Angharad smiled gently at his wistful expression.

"I suppose it's only reasonable a baby should have priority," she laughed. "Darling... children are more important than material things, we are allowed to change our minds, you know, there's nothing to stop us doing that." One lazy Saturday morning a few weeks later, Angharad picked up the post from the doormat and opening a letter addressed to her said,

"They've booked me a bed in St. David's maternity ward. Darling it's really happening!" She giggled and threw her arms around his neck, planting a kiss firmly on his lips. Peering closely at the other letter in her hand she smiled,

"One for you from the old country." He slit the envelope and withdrew an invitation from his old grammar school to speak on the occasion of their annual prize-giving.

Two years previously, Patrick had organised for children from Catholic and Protestant areas of Belfast to holiday together in Wales. He believed passionately, that only with the help of such arrangements, would the two sides come together and begin to understand one another. His old school, knowing about this, were providing him with a platform to advertise and tell them all about it.

That night all the foreboding that Angharad had felt during her visit to Belfast returned. Unable to sleep, she sat beside the window, looking out over the mountains until they were bathed in the dawn light. Patrick had lost his heart here but his ties with Ireland would always be strong. He lay peaceful in sleep and she studied his face in the moonlight which slanted in through the curtains. It was fine boned, his features so clear cut that she wished she was a sculptor, able to create something as beautiful.

"Please don't accept that invitation," she begged next morning. "I have an awful feeling about it darling, it really worries me."

"Oh you and your second sight," he laughed, "I'll only be there for a few days." She knew there was no dissuading him, appreciating the deep passions he felt. He called the divide in his country the "religious rape" of the people and he wasn't usually given to florid language. Waving to him as the ferry departed, she shivered, frightened by a certainty that something evil was riding free. He had tried in vain to persuade her to go with him. However, she didn't want to experience that awful feeling of foreboding again while she was pregnant. She was sure that stress could affect the baby she was carrying. It was a ridiculous decision really, because she was feeling stressed anyway. She didn't sleep that night and the next day passed slowly. She felt cold and detached, barely speaking to anyone.

When the police came to the door of Rush Cottage they were surprised by her reaction. There was a lack of emotion and something else which they couldn't comprehend. They were not unused to breaking bad news, but her silent, tearless acceptance was something more than just shock. They notified her doctor and he agreed there was something not quite normal, considering the circumstances. He arrived at the cottage to see Angharad sitting beside the radio, white faced and unmoving. She seemed not to know he was there, didn't respond when he spoke. Mindful of the unborn child, he felt he had to get through to Angharad somehow, had to break down that invisible barrier. She needed to express her grief, to cry, scream, throw something. Anything was preferable to this contained withdrawal. He went to switch the radio off and as he did so the news headlines were read for the umpteenth time that day.

"The man killed in an explosion earlier today in the centre of Belfast, has been named as Mr. Patrick Rush. Mr. Rush who was Irish and married, has been living in North Wales where he worked as a teacher. He was visiting Belfast to speak at the prize giving ceremony in his old school. No one has yet claimed responsibility for this latest act of terrorism."

Dr.Rhys watched anxiously for any sign that Angharad was hearing the bulletin. There was only the tiniest flicker of her eyelids.

"You must get some rest," he said taking her arm and gently leading her towards her bedroom. Sedation and careful nursing was the only answer. He was totally unprepared for what happened. Tearing free from his guiding hand, Angharad raced across the room and out of the front door. Before he could catch her she was running down the path.

“My God.” He shouted but he was too late. She was through the gate in a trice and the car hit her a glancing blow as she ran straight into its path. The driver swerved to avoid a collision, his momentum carried him up the grass verge on the wrong side of the road and he ended up in the ditch. Bruised and shaken he scrambled out, protesting,

“I didn't see her, she came out of nowhere?” Dr. Rhys could vouch for that but he was busy examining Angharad, thankful to find that there were no broken bones as far as he could tell. The big question was the baby. The neighbours had heard the crash and doors to the other cottages were opened as they came running out to see what had happened. More people gathered as they always do when there is an accident and soon ambulance and police arrived.

Angharad had been grief stricken for months afterwards. She felt there was nothing left, no Patrick, no child. She lost interest in everything and the little house they had been so happy to work on was left with an unpainted nursery and an unfinished kitchen. She couldn’t continue working at the library, meeting happy people every day, she wanted the time to herself. The decision to turn her hobby of pottery design into a small business seemed to be a success, for four or five years, but then as the business began to slide all her old doubts and sorrows returned, leaving her depressed and anxious.

Grace Jones let herself into the cottage and noted the smashed pottery.”

“Oh, my God Angharad, 'tis trouble isn't it?” She dropped her bag and ran to comfort her daughter. “Now you tell me all about it,” she fell back easily into the manner she had used when the children were small.

“I'm alright now Mam. I've had a good cry. I was just feeling sorry for myself... and angry... for destroying all I had left of Patrick. Oh mam, if only I hadn’t lost the baby.” She began to sob again with her mother's arms around her.

“He would be a growing lad by now my dear and that would double your worries now, wouldn't it? You haven’t made any money this year. How would you be able to feed a hungry seven year old?” Angharad sat up with a start, realising that her mother's thoughts must often dwell on the lost baby too. Naturally she grieved for the grandchild she had been denied. She, Angharad, wasn't the only one to have suffered a loss, yet here she was indulging in self pity. Hugging her mother, she dried her tears and took a deep breath.

“One thing's for sure... I'll not make a living this way. Let's have a coffee and give some more thought to that idea of yours. What do you think I could sell in a Country Goods Store?”

14. NETTA

Dave pulled in to the lay-by which also served as a bus stop. Back in the thirties, a row of semi-detached houses had signalled the start of Bangor's urban growth. The houses were lower than the road so several steps climbed up to the gates of each one. Dave noticed Netta standing with one hand on her gate and puffing from her exertions. He stopped right alongside her, pressed the door button and she waddled across to the bus.

"Hello Dave," she greeted him, breathless but smiling. "I just timed that right," she laughed hauling herself up and into the bus. She smiled at the other passengers, noticing a smartly dressed, good looking lad with a surly expression, arm curled round an expensive looking brief case. He wasn't the usual type of passenger she thought and wondered who he was. Taking a seat behind Dave, she extracted her purse from a huge handbag. She had known Dave since childhood; they had lived next door to each other in Dyffryn village, a mile west of Troed-y-Rhiw. They had been to the same schools and attended the same chapel.

"Bus station, please Dave," she said still panting. He automatically gave her a return ticket and taking her change from him she settled back in the seat. Dave steered away from the lay-by and began the final part of the journey. He drove past the old football field and Regal Cinema, now a Bingo Hall where he picked up a few more passengers, then along Station road and past the University before pulling in to the bus station and parking in the number eleven bay. He jumped down from his cab and went round to help his passengers alight. He nodded and smiled as they descended, some eager, some as though they had all day, others like Herb Rowlands with obvious difficulty. Netta waited until last because she was unable to manoeuvre with any semblance of speed. Dave helped her to the tarmac and then checked through the bus. He wasn't surprised to find a canvas bag which he recognised as belonging to one of the shop assistants.

He locked the vehicle, handed the carrier-bag in to the 'Lost Property Office' and five minutes later was enjoying a cup of tea in the canteen when his boss came over.

"Heard about the old lady.... from the cottages above Glasfryn?" He whistled the question through the gap in his front teeth.

"Found in her back yard this morning..... broken hip and exposure.... been there for hours I believe...." He broke off seeing the look on Dave's face.

"I saw the ambulance, but didn't know where it was going of course," Dave said.

"Name of Parry…" his boss began.

"Mary Jane. I know her... oh dear... poor soul," Dave was distressed. "But she's Elwyn Rhys's aunt... did you know?"

That's why I'm here, looking for someone to take his shift. He was down for this afternoon, but he just phoned in from the hospital..." He scratched his thinning hairline, looking worried.

"Don't worry, I'll do his shift. Be sure to let me know if you have any news." Dave finished his tea and re-scheduling his day in his mind, went to phone his wife.

After Netta Thomas gratefully accepted Dave's help, she buttoned her coat, pulled down her woolly hat and grasped her handbag to her ample form. Ready at last, she headed up the hill with a determination matched only by the Tensings and Hilary's of this world.

She always hated the climb from the bus station; it left her sweating and panting before she even began her round of the shops. She had come into Bangor on the early bus because she was going to the hairdresser. As her appointment wasn't due for almost half an hour she headed for 'The Welsh Lady' tea-rooms. A cup of coffee would be nice before submitting to the tortures of permanent waving.

The cafe was an offshoot of a local bakery. In the afternoons, most of Bangor's elderly female population could be found there, enjoying a cup of tea and exchanging the latest gossip. This early in the morning however, the waitresses were still busy setting the tables and arranging cakes on the trolley.

A cup of coffee was set unceremoniously in front of her and the girl hurried away to the kitchen. She reappeared a few minutes later with a plate of scones which she placed on the trolley beside a chocolate gateau. Netta eyed the scones which her nostrils told her were fresh and warm from the oven and in vain she tried to resist. Calling the girl over she said she would like one.

"Butter or cream?" the waitress asked.

Netta stirred brown sugar into her coffee while scone, cream and strawberry jam were placed on her table.

Exactly twenty minutes later she entered the already humid atmosphere of 'Hairlyne'. The manager resplendent in grey suit and pink tie welcomed her with a flourish, took her coat and showed her to a seat in the waiting area. She looked round at the girls who all appeared slim and smartly dressed although one or two had hairstyles more reminiscent of storks nests. She would not have thought them good adverts for the business, but glancing at the wall posters, had to admit the hair on the models bore a definite resemblance.

A youth with skin like a fresh peach stood beside her, cape in hand.

"Will you have the backwash madam?" he wanted to know. Netta didn't like to be different by saying she would prefer to sit forward, so she let him show her to the row of shell pink wash-bowls with their neck rests clamped ready behind the chairs. He wrapped towels around her neck and she shuffled her bulk down into the crimson, vinyl seat. As the youth moved away, Llinor, her regular hairdresser greeted her.

"Same as usual?" She asked, not expecting a negative reply. Netta didn't surprise her, unable to imagine what else she could do with her thinning locks. She liked to have a regular perm although she dreaded most of the stages necessary to achieve results. There were the rollers that pulled, the unpleasant smell which sometimes made her retch and the painful combing out of tangled locks. Today proved no exception and it was with considerable relief that she paid her bill a few hours later. Her throat was parched after sitting under the dryer and there were distinct rumbles from her middle region. She headed once again for 'The Welsh Lady' tea rooms, anticipation of a tasty meal adding urgency to her footsteps.

The lunch hour rush had started, but there was one free table squashed in a corner beside the toilet door and the coat hooks. It was a challenging business getting herself installed there and she found herself on the receiving end of black looks and sour comments as she made her way between the tables. Embarrassed, she studied the menu with unnecessary attention choosing plaice, chips and peas with tea and a cake to follow.

"I'll diet tomorrow," she said to herself, tucking in with guilty resignation. She had lost count of the times she had repeated the intention and she knew she wouldn't keep to her vow. She was so weak willed and how she hated herself for it. Sometimes she consoled herself that it was all a matter of genes. Their distribution certainly hadn't come down kindly in her case, for she took after her father's rotund family. On her mother's side they were all like broomsticks, could eat anything and simply never put on weight. Her brother was blessed with the maternal inheritance.

The fish was fresh and the chips beautifully crisp and brown. Afterwards she chose a piece of Battenburg cake, took a knife and separated the four quarters, savouring each in turn. When she had finished she drank her tea and studied her shopping list.

"Hello Netta, how are you?" Jenny Peters stood beside her, looking neat and bright as usual. "We've just been to the hospital to see little Danny... so hot there, we're parched. I'm dyin' for a cup of tea." She sat down opposite, but before Netta could ask after the baby she carried on speaking.

"Little Danny's doing so well, bless him... put on just over a pound. They reckon he should be strong enough to go home in about three weeks. Oh it's a shame it is... poor little soul... all those tubes and everything."

"Oh mam, don't keep on," Sheila joined them with one of her other children beside her. "Look, I want to nip up to the post office... can I park Keith here with you? I'll only be as long as it takes." Jenny Peters beamed brightly at her daughter.

"Of course you can my dear, no hurry, we'll be fine won't we Keith?" She lifted the toddler on to her knee, while Sheila warned her not to spoil his appetite for tea at home.

Netta and Jenny fell into easy chatter, they too had known each other since school days and had many mutual friends. Jenny asked,

"Have you heard about Mrs. Parry... Glasfryn? Rushed to the C and A this morning with a broken hip. Someone said she fell down outside, soaked she was... terrible isn't it? Poor thing. We called at orthopaedic on our way out and asked after her...couldn't see her... she was in surgery."

The waitress pulled a spare chair towards them and asked Keith if he would like to sit in it. She lifted him on to it.

"Be like a big man," she said, smiling and winking as she put a glass of orange and a chocolate biscuit in front of him. While they gossiped, they had tea and cakes and by the time Sheila returned, protesting at the length of post office queues, Netta was beginning to feel anxious about the time so she excused herself and left to do her shopping.

"Maybe see you on the bus," Jenny called after her.

Dave was sitting in his seat waiting till it was time to drive back in the direction of Cwm Wylfa. He was beginning to see some of his earlier passengers returning. Jenny was not on the bus but Herb Rowlands was. Netta tried to start a conversation, but he seemed disinclined to talk, lost in his own little world. She always felt rather sorry for him, wondering how he managed, living alone, doing everything for himself especially with those hands. Terribly deformed they were, he couldn't hold things properly. Such an awful thing, arthritis. She'd heard stories about him in the war but no one seemed to know for certain what was true and what wasn't. Somehow it never seemed right to ask about things like that. When Dave stopped opposite the lay-by, Netta rose from her seat and struggled to leave the bus, weighed down with a heavy carrier bag.

By the time she had descended the steps, entered her house and put the shopping away she was exhausted. A cup of coffee and a short rest was necessary before preparing the evening meal. She took out the semi-skimmed milk, pleased that they had both become used to it. It was supposed to be healthier than full cream, but usually she and Bryn found these 'so called' healthy foods unpalatable one way or another.

Bryn refused to go without salt in spite of his doctor's advice. She was a bit anxious about it because he did have very high blood pressure as well as doing all kinds of things he was advised not to do. He went to work in the car, sat for hours at his desk doing a minimum of teaching now that he was headmaster, but suffering a lot of strain and stress from the administrative part of the job.

"Nothing but a ruddy office clerk these days," he complained with regularity. His evenings were spent watching television and the most energetic thing he ever did was to wash the car or mow the little bit of grass they called a garden. Netta shrugged. There was no easy way to change one's habits, especially when they were well into middle age.

She was pleased to have seen Jenny Peters, but wished she had not eaten another cake while they chatted. Jenny had nodded in the direction of the trolley, groaning under its load of home baking and Netta's resistance had crumbled. But she derived such comfort from her indulgence, so why should she feel guilty about it? Her own family didn't help.

"No wonder you don't lose weight, eating that sort of thing." It was always the young ones who made these remarks in a superior 'wouldn't you think she'd know better at her age' sort of tone. It was alright for them dashing about here and there, they never had a chance to put on weight. She had been like that herself when she was younger but now she never had the energy to do more than keep the house tidy and cook the meals.

She drained her coffee, rinsed the mug and put the milk back in the fridge. As she did so her eye fell on the remains of yesterday's chocolate cake.

Only one piece left, too small to share with Bryn. No one around to criticize so she polished it off while she put away the few items she had bought in the shops. She looked at her watch, almost lost in the tissue of fat around her wrist: gone four, which meant Bryn would be home soon. She put the kettle ready and sliced the fruit cake she had brought back from Bangor.

She really must diet, she could not go on like this, but how did one find the will power to stick to it? She thought of all the times she had started out full of good intent. Years ago, Bryn had built a shelf for her cookery books, but she had collected far more books on diets. There were crash diets and diets for life, fruit diets and liquid diets. There was a fibre diet book and the "Pear-shaped People's Diet". There were diet supplements from magazines and a scrap book she had compiled herself. Weightwatchers recipes had seen their turn too. She had tried everything at one time or another, yet here she was, seven years later and over four stones too heavy.

Sighing, she began to peel the potatoes. They were going to have cold ham and parsley sauce tonight. Should they have peas or carrots, or both? She sliced the ham which she had boiled the day before. It was a lovely piece, really tasty and so tender that it was crumbling when she tried to slice it thin. Absent mindedly she gathered up the broken pieces and ate them.

Bryn had asked her to repair a shirt, so picking it up together with her work-basket she wandered through to the living room. From habit she switched on the radio, but turned her attention to the shirt. Gradually the B.B.C. voice insinuated itself into her mind. She paid full attention now, annoyed that she had been only half listening before. It was something about older women suffering from brittle bones. Osteo-something did he say? Need calcium... found in dairy foods... but surely? Oh dear, her mind was in turmoil, did that mean she shouldn't be drinking skimmed milk after all? Did that mean cream cakes were actually good for her?

Later she broached the subject with Bryn, and then wished she hadn't. He reminded her of her lack of will power, and said she had to face up to the fact that she was fat. They may as well both enjoy decent food, he said, and stop worrying about diets. She couldn't understand why his attitude disappointed her so. Was it because he didn't appear particularly interested? She sensed that her size embarrassed him, yet he didn't make any effort to help.

She sighed, Bryn wasn't interested in anything these days and consequently he was no company. Conversation was rare, as he was either in front of the box or sitting over a pile of school work. The intimate side of their life had been non-existent for years and they just lived together in a semi-detached silence most of the time. She sighed again and burped discreetly; Bryn had fallen asleep and the television was talking to itself. She changed channels, found a programme more to her liking, put her feet up and fished around in her bag for a peppermint.

15. HERB

After saying farewell to Netta, the bus reached the trading estate outside Happistores, where a crowd of pensioners loaded with 'Discount Day' groceries boarded the bus. Albert waved from his kiosk in the car park as the bus pulled away from the stop. They went past a garage, a dilapidated looking pub with boarded up windows that had not dodged the graffiti vandals. Next came an expanse of waste ground with a notice announcing that it had been acquired for development and then they were back at the Golden Fleece. Ahead in the distance on the slope of the hill, some newly built 'executive' houses looked out over the half finished comprehensive school. Beyond them, the wooded slopes which bordered the Peris estate masked the two famous bridges spanning the Menai Straits.

Dave drove on to the stop and waited patiently while Herb negotiated his way down the steps, then with a cheery "Hwyl" he waved and shut the door. A glance into his wing mirror showed a motor bike coming up at speed behind him so he waited for it to go past before he signalled and pulled away from the kerbside. Some motorbike that was, he thought enviously as it roared past with a deep throaty reverberation, it would cost every bit as much as a car if you tried to buy one. He had seen it around once or twice before today, so he supposed it belonged to some newcomer to the area. He recalled some German tourists on the Holyhead ferry with big bikes like that. They were comparative youngsters and he was surprised that they could afford such machines.

He remembered the thrill when he bought his own bike. He found it in a scrap yard and purchased it with bits and pieces of others. Then he spent every spare moment rebuilding it and hadn't done a bad job, at least it got him around for a few years. He never got the big, new one he promised himself because before that happened he fell in love. Faith didn't like motor bikes and anyway they were no good for transporting young families.

Earlier that morning when the bus had arrived in Bangor, Herb Rowlands had stepped off with difficulty: his knees wouldn't work as they should these days. Smart in his tweed suit and with brogues polished like ripe apples, he had steadied himself with the aid of his stick and contemplated the walk up into the town. He felt particularly frail these days especially when he was in a crowd, so he picked his way carefully. People in a hurry, pushchairs and exuberant children were studiously avoided lest they knocked against him and upset his balance. He found himself ever more dependent on his walking stick as the feeling of vertigo became more insistent. Happily, he found the supermarket trolley a useful support and the store stocked everything on his list.

Afterwards, weighed down with a shopping bag in one hand, he had walked close to the buildings and made his way slowly to the public library. There as he did every week, he had enjoyed a few hours of warmth and comfort among the local history books. Emerging into the street again and turning towards the bus station, he stopped suddenly as a familiar figure walked past him. His heart began to thump so strongly it was almost painful. It was impossible, he knew that, but he stood shaken, staring in disbelief after the young man. He reminded him so much of Eric.

On the bus home, he found his thoughts constantly returning to the encounter. It was a painful experience seeing such an uncanny resemblance to that handsome face with its boyish grin, remembering the charm, the stubborn determination and the frightening idealism. Eric was a part of his past which he considered best forgotten, but try as he might, he could not switch his mind to other matters.

Back home he was still in a state of shock. Behaving like some kind of automaton he reached for the kettle, over-filled it with water and switched it on. Only when it spluttered did he wrench his thoughts back to the present. Making a pot of tea he decided to spoil himself and added a dash of rum. He put the tea-pot on the trolley and steered into his small sitting room, parking it beside his chair. He lowered himself gently into the cushions, hooked the footstool nearer and carefully lifted his feet on to it. Weary but comfortable now, he was able to relax and allow his thoughts and feelings to take over.

Eric and he, although born in Dyllas a few miles from Troed-y-Rhiw, had grown up together on a large Friesland farm. Their mother, widowed when they were baby and toddler, could hardly believe her good fortune when Jan Kloos, a holidaying Dutchman, swept her into a second, incredibly happy marriage. Aged four and six when they went to live in Holland, very soon the only noticeably Welsh thing about the boys was their birth father's name.

Jan was a marvellous stepfather. He always had time for the pair of them, in spite of the demands of work on the farm. He involved them in what he was doing, giving them a feeling of importance, and a sense of responsibility. They helped with the milking and cleaning out the large 'schuur' where the cows were housed in winter. They enjoyed many an hour romping in the fields with Rodi the dog, or riding the horses, bareback.

Jan never allowed them to forget that they were Welsh. Even though they grew up considering themselves to be Dutch, he insisted that their mother speak to them in Welsh, he even learned it himself. Every year he made sure she returned to Wales with them to visit family and friends. Herb looked forward to these holidays. He loved the open landscape of Friesland, but something Welsh in his soul attracted him to the mountains.

As they grew up, their different characters asserted themselves. He, was the quieter, being rather introverted and self critical. He took life seriously, but didn't lack a sense of humour. Often he and Eric would see the funny side of something and indulge in fits of giggling. Jan would pretend to be cross at their tomfoolery.

“Stop this 'dwaasheid' and get on with your job,” he would chide.

“I'll have to knock some sense into you,” he would threaten, rolling up his sleeves and making playful lunges in their direction. Inevitably they ducked and responded and five or ten minutes of horseplay followed.

Sometimes their mother despaired of them, for all three would be quite oblivious to their surroundings when the fun started. More often than not, it took place in the muck of the barn or the mud of the fields. All of it before the days of washing machines! He conjured up his mother's patient expression as she resigned herself to the task ahead on wash-day.

Herb reached for his tea, smiling to himself as he remembered one particular occasion. He and Jan had joined in teasing Eric who was boasting of his prowess on skates. Jan insisted that they were given proof of his newly acquired talent. Knowing that the ice was not as thick as it looked, he had winked at Herb, and led the way to the farm pond, a large but shallow stretch of water in the corner of a field. Here Eric had launched himself eagerly with the intention of demonstrating his talent. Instead, there had been a loud crack and he had descended into three feet of icy water as Jan had fully intended he should.

Eric had always been the lively one. He was good at skating as later events proved. He came second in the 'Elfstedentocht' when he was only seventeen. The race, over two hundred kilometers of frozen canals and through eleven towns could not have been better proof of his talent and stamina. There had been a great sense of pride in the family after that event.

After leaving school, Herb worked on the farm until he left for University in Groningen, but it was while he was engrossed in his studies that two things happened to change his life. First, Germany attacked Poland, then Britain declared war. There was great consternation throughout the rest of Europe and at home his mother was concerned for her relatives and friends back in Wales.

Herb hadn't known what to do. There was talk of Holland remaining neutral, but people didn't like to speculate. They pushed politics into the background and whenever they could, changed the subject. Discussion at the University was lively. Sadly, a certain faction allied itself with the German fascists and became very militant in belief and behaviour. Its membership was small in number, but it was an odious presence.

When Herb returned to the farm for a weekend, it was to find an atmosphere very different from the usual carefree magic. Jan was surprisingly taciturn and his mother though happy to see him, appeared uneasy. It was when he tackled Eric, that he received the biggest shock. They were working together, clearing out one of the drainage ditches and he asked Eric why Jan and their mother were apparently so distraught. Eric shrugged his shoulders in an offhand manner.

“I suppose I'm the reason. I can't see eye to eye with them these days. The only person with whom I have anything at all in common is Kor van de Boer. We both agree that the fascist doctrine is the only one you can really admire. Look at the way Hitler has tackled his country's economic problems: the Germans absolutely idolise him. No one has done so much for his country as he has. When I went to Berlin last Easter, I couldn't help but admire everything. There was a kind of subdued excitement with everyone busy building a New Germany. They were proud and rightly so. D'you know ...?” and Eric launched into a long, involved, personal appraisal of all that he had seen.

Herb had been utterly dismayed to see Eric in this latest persona, but he knew from experience at the University, that the fascists were a plausible lot. He had almost been taken in himself, but it was after a pleasant evening celebrating his birthday with friends in a local bar that he had been disenchanted. Walking beside the canal and about to cross one of the many bridges they had seen something hanging above the water. Closer inspection revealed that it was a youth about their own age who had been badly beaten up and then regardless of injury, bound hand and foot and suspended by a rope from the centre of the bridge. Horrified that anyone could treat another human being in such a way, they rescued the lad, removed his bindings and carried him to a doctor where they heard the full, sad story.

He was the son of a Jewish lawyer in the town. A group of fascists had earlier that week wrecked the man's office and threatened his family. They had waylaid the boy on his return home from a music lesson. His bicycle and violin had been thrown into the canal before they set on him. Sickened, Herb had decided there and then that if he was ever called upon to fight fascism, he would do so willingly. Eric had shrugged his shoulders and said it was only what Jews deserved.

The rest of his weekend at home had been miserable. He'd tried for everyone's sake to dissuade Eric from his new frightening obsession. It was apparent however, that the harder he tried, the more determined Eric became. Looking back, he often despaired, knowing that it was most probable he had been the catalyst. He had finally driven Eric into the hands of the fascists, by simply attempting to turn him in the opposite direction. Jan and their mother, appreciating the stubborn streak in Eric had refrained from discussing politics. They feared doing precisely what Herb had in all innocence achieved.

Kor van de Boer had begun work on the farm when Herb first left for university. He had proved a major influence on Eric, the impressionable teenager toiling alongside him in the school holidays. Eric who had originally intended following his brother to University, had gradually inclined more to joining the army. But it was not the army of his adopted country that he wished to help, nor that of his birthplace. Encouraged by Kor, Eric had become a member of the National Socialist Movement, and it was there he found an outlet for his energy and enthusiasm. That fateful weekend, Kor had left the farm and taken a willing Eric with him.

Herb hadn't returned to University. Heavy with guilt for the part he felt he had played in Eric's departure, he stayed to help run the farm. The three of them lived together harmoniously enough, but the air was tainted. Eric had been lost to what they instinctively felt to be an evil cause. It was bigger than any of them and something they couldn't fight and expect to win.

Jan suddenly became an old man. He moved around the farm like a shadow and he no longer laughed. Herb's mother also went about quietly with a certain resignation and a droop to her shoulders. Tactfully questioned she would answer,

“I don't think he'll come back. I know he's still young, easily swayed, but

... Eric always craved excitement and now he's getting it."

The following May, Holland was invaded and within days had surrendered to the might of the German Reich. Rather than be compromised into working for the Germans, Herb decided to go into hiding. With his nation now irretrievably involved in the war Jan regained something of his former spirit. He and Herb excavated a hiding place beneath the barn floor. There, made comfortable with furnishings from the house, Herb decided to conceal himself, when just before Christmas he received instructions to join a work party, travelling to Germany. Soldiers came to the farm to know why he hadn't reported. Jan and his mother with an assumed air of bewilderment said that he had left home with the intention of doing so, promising to report if he returned. Jan, was allowed a special dispensation, for he, like many farmers was required to work on the land.

So began the dangerous years. In time, a resistance network grew up and they were able to contact the British who supplied them with sabotage equipment, the R.A.F. dropping everything by parachute in pre-arranged places. Eventually it fell to Herb to organise these dropping zones and get useful information out. He rarely moved by day because the countryside was so open that it didn't afford much cover. At odd times, when the drainage ditches were dry, he could move with comparative ease. He savoured these rare excursions in the fresh daylight air.

Life on the farm continued with the constrictions imposed by occupation the only change to routine. Being a farm, they fared better with food than people in the cities and Jan stocked up Herb's food supply whenever he felt safe from prying eyes. The 'den' was reasonably well ventilated, but Herb often yearned to get out of its stifling atmosphere. Occasionally, he was joined by R.A.F. men, his secret room just one of many on their escape route.

Unfortunately quislings exist and someone betrayed him. One moonlit night at the end of February 1944, he was awakened by shouts, shots and running booted feet. Hauled roughly from his hiding place, he was dragged past the bloodied bodies of Jan and his mother. They lay where their lives had ended, beneath the wall of their beloved farm. He was thrown into a guarded truck and taken to the local S.S. headquarters. They had questioned and threatened, starved and bullied, but he had given nothing away. Then they tried a change of tactics. The cell door opened and admitted Eric.

He could picture him now, tall, healthy and smart in the hated uniform. With a supercilious look his brother had taunted him, calling him stupid. He should have joined the Nationalist Movement, gone with him in the beginning. Eric told how he had travelled to Germany, with other members of the group and after a short while had been taken under the wing of an influential fascist family.

"Herr Scholtz has been a father to me," he smiled. "He even suggested that I adopt his name... to help me become a true German... and now I have a beautiful German wife as well." Herb, his heart heavy, and weak from the torture he had received, could only spit in the direction of Eric's polished boots,

"Traitor." A shadow of distaste crossed his brother's face, but he leaned forward and with a glimmer of his boyhood self urged,

"You must answer their questions. You know we will win in the end, so save yourself more pain." Herb had sneered at this. It was common knowledge that the Germans were losing the war and the allies were marching relentlessly across Europe.

That was the last time he had seen Eric. When the ploy of brotherly persuasion hadn't worked, he had been loaded with other prisoners into an army truck for what was presumably intended to be his final trip. Their journey was interrupted by heavy shelling from the allies who had moved more quickly than the Germans had anticipated. The truck was caught in a blast and it careered off the road, hit a tree and fell on to its side over a ditch. The front was crushed, the canvas cover on the back ripped off and bodies spilled out into a heap. A machine gun opened up and sprayed the human pile. Miraculously, Herb was unhurt. He lay beneath the other prisoners in the bottom of the ditch. Anyone who moved or groaned was shot immediately. One of the bullets gauged out a deep wound along Herb's arm. A few inches to the side and it could have been fatal. He lay still, heart beating, praying that the soldiers wouldn't investigate too closely. The small stream at the bottom of the ditch was cold and did nothing to help his situation as it gradually soaked his clothing from head to foot. As evening fell and the shelling subsided he sized up the situation, and took his chance. German troops had been passing by all day but it had been quiet for a time. Wary lest he make a careless mistake, he carefully extricated himself from beneath his fellow prisoners. Practised in the art of using ditches for cover, he reached the Canadian lines safely. They dispatched him to the nearest hospital and after discharge some time later, he was transported to the British army lines. They in turn got him back to England from where he made his way to North Wales.

He had a cousin in Dyllas and another in Bangor, but each had lost a son and touched by these tragedies of war they were somewhat detached, the former warmth had gone out of the relationship. The one exception had been Auntie Mair who was a wise old bird and kind. She gave him a home and in return he helped in her tiny village shop at Troed-y-Rhiw. He was never very fit, his imprisonment having left him with an inheritance of pain, but she showed compassion and understanding whenever he was depressed. She was also a great comfort when sleep was shattered by nightmares that would not dissipate, even in the light of dawn.

When Auntie Mair died, she left him her home the shop and all that she had in the way of savings. It wasn't a fortune, but it was enough to estrange him finally from the rest of the family. He had never been back to the farm in Friesland. He didn't believe that he had the mental stamina to go there and inevitably re-live the horrific events. He preferred to picture in his mind the earlier, happy days of his childhood.

The telephone crashed into his reverie. He reached out with difficulty, lifting the receiver in his deformed hand. His heart thumped uncomfortably as he listened to the young man's voice.

"My name is Franz ... Franz Scholtz. I am only now in Wales. Please, I call at your home? Father require that I find you. My grandfather ... I do not know him, he was in the war killed ... His name was Eric."

16. GWILYM

He had slowed the little train for the level crossing at Troed-y-Rhiw and Gwilym could see that Jane Evans was taking her time opening the gates, as usual. He swore to himself, knowing that she did it on purpose. He moved to the other side of the tiny cab, leaned out and looked back along the line. Sure enough he was just in time to see the disappearing rump of a schoolboy in a doorway of the fifth carriage.

For the umpteenth time he considered getting his own back and making Jane Evans wait for once. Unfortunately, that would also mean holding up the traffic while he walked the length of the train to turn the boys off. Seeing a traffic queue building up, his courage deserted him.

He swallowed his annoyance once more, released the brake and 'Prince Llewellyn' rolled gently over the crossing. He raised his fist to Jane Evans as he passed. Her response was a toothy grin from beneath the hair-net and a deep laugh which echoed after him.

It had been a daily occurrence since the holiday crowds had thinned. When the afternoon train approached the crossing, he would sound the whistle and slow down as the rules demanded, but Jane Evans' leisurely pace would make it necessary to stop. Seizing their opportunity, about half a dozen lads just out of the nearby school, would sneak in to the simple wooden carriages and steal a free ride. He might have shut his eyes to their behaviour had it not been for a cigarette butt which he had found one day smouldering beneath a seat. He felt sure they were the culprits. Now he felt more concerned for the safety of the train than in humouring a few naughty boys. With her toothy grin Jane Evans smiled at the drivers of the various vehicles on the road and slowly shuffled across to close the second gate. When Gwilym had taken the train over the crossing she slowly reversed the procedure.

Dave, his philosophic nature unruffled, sat patiently waiting. He acknowledged Gwilym's wave from the tiny cab and with amusement watched the expressions of the tourists in the carriages as they noticed Jane Evans. Her ruddy complexion, netted, grey locks and ample figure always drew attention. She knew it and enjoyed it, standing with her great beefy arms akimbo as the little train puffed out of sight round the hillside.

Three miles further on Gwilym sounded the whistle again as he ran into the station. He braked, jumped out and hurried back to the fifth carriage. Anticipating his move, the boys scattered and disappeared before he could remonstrate with them. He joined the guard, who was watching passengers alight. Because he was lame from a quarry accident, Glyn knew he had no chance of catching errant schoolboys.

"Bin fairly busy today," Glyn commented leaning against the side of the guards van. With amusement they watched two young railway enthusiasts, each about six feet tall, unfold themselves from the half-size coaches. They were rubbing their bottoms, numb from an hour on the slatted wooden seats. Families with sticky children gathered round the steaming engine, chattering, pointing and taking photographs.

"Well all to the good. Better get his highness into the shed. See you tomorrow Glyn." Gwilym bent over so that he could walk through the carriages towards the engine, glancing in all the corners as he passed. No lost property and no smouldering cigarettes this time. He chatted for a few minutes with the children and their parents, answering their questions, then he warned them to stand clear and watched with amusement as they jumped clear of the spurt of steam emanating from the piston as he moved away.

The last run of the day was over and he was tired. He disconnected the carriages, drove the engine into the shed, raked out the fire and locked up. He felt his age these days and found it increasingly difficult to keep going as he once had. Bright and early next morning, he must stoke the boiler, polish the brass work and get ready for another crowd of tourists.

Carlo sat beside the cottage door, bright eyed and eager, greeting his master with a great show of affection. Gwilym called hello to Betty who was busy cooking in the little back kitchen and throwing off his cap sank into the chair that had been his father's before him. The dog sat at his feet and rested one paw in his lap.

Gwilym shut his eyes, remembering the time when he and his father were both employed by the quarry, taking trains carrying slate to the dock at Blaen-y-Nant. On the return journeys they carried spare parts, fuel and occasionally an unauthorised passenger. He and his father were good friends and rarely had a cross word.

When his father retired, Gwilym spent the evenings keeping him abreast of quarry news and gossip. He was slow to find the girl he wanted to marry, but when he did Betty came to live in the cottage and like a daughter, looked after the old man till his time too, had run out. They were never blessed with children and that was their only sadness in life.

Gradually times changed, there was less demand for slate and the quarry began to fail. Gwilym was no economist and never really understood all the problems. He carried on working as long as he was allowed, every week seeing more of his friends laid off with no prospect of alternative employment. Eventually his turn came and he locked the little engines into the shed for the last time.

He and Betty worried about their home, unsure how they stood concerning the tenancy. There were two more houses in their terrace which were occupied. One was home to Nan Jones an elderly widow and the other to the Prichard family of five. Everyone expected to be told to leave, because property owners were making big money selling local cottages. Incomers bought them, refurbished them and then often used them only for holidays. It caused much bad feeling because it priced local people out of the housing market, a particularly sad situation for first time buyers. It was happening all over Wales and a militant group decided to protest by burning down some of these homes, so Gwilym and Betty kept a wary eye on the empty properties in their terrace.

Rumours abounded, but to everyone's surprise they were never told to move and stranger still, after a week or so of the quarry closing down, no one came to collect the rent. On two occasions, unknown business men appeared at the door and discussed ownership of the houses and possible rent charges, but nothing more happened.

Nan Jones moved to an old folk’s home a couple of years later and the Prichard family moved to a council house. It was nearly seven years after this that the railway and bordering land was acquired by a big, well established leisure group. The company insisted that it was necessary to modernise all the buildings including their cottage, but the rent they intended to charge afterwards was one which Gwilym and Betty could not afford. Over the years when no one collected, they had set aside the usual rent, for fear that one day they would be asked to pay the arrears. Unfortunately, they had dipped into this fund over the years as repairs became necessary to keep the place habitable. Now with little more than their pension money, the rent that they were facing was far beyond them. Sadly, for they did not want to leave their home, they put their name on a council housing list. After three or four weeks of uncertainty, a company representative appeared at the door and explained,

"The railway is to be re-opened as a tourist attraction, we need someone to drive the train, someone who has experience. We wondered if you would be interested, you act as driver in exchange for a reduction in rent." Gwilym, thrilled at his change of luck accepted the offer straight away.

The rest of their terrace was re-designed to include ticket-office, store, souvenir shop and cafe. It also formed the Troed-y-Rhiw railway station terminus, because the quayside where they had once unloaded, a mile or so further on, was now a housing estate. Back near the quarry the line bordered the lake and climbed to just over a thousand feet where it entered the old workings through one of the original tunnels. Here, visitors could wander round the museum, walk along the line and see the old inclines and various work-sheds and offices. Gwilym often wondered what his father would make of the situation. He would never have visualised people with time and money to spare, paying to ride on his railway. He always thought of it as his railway.

On the day the new tourist attraction opened Gwilym stood proudly at the controls of the "Padarn Castle", its brass gleaming and paintwork shining as they steamed out of the station. Flowers and flags decorated the coaches and people at the trackside threw streamers and cheered as they watched the train go by.

Beside Gwilym and unbelievably dirty in greasy overalls stood Peter, Lord Peris, whose help had done much to get the project launched. His father, the original owner of the quarry, had always lived in London, only occasionally showing up at his estate for the fishing, but Peter proved to be very different. After obtaining his degree at Cambridge, he settled in the family home, starting up a light engineering business on the estate. The old stables became offices and workrooms and he made a point of employing local people when possible. He became a familiar and popular figure in the district, enjoying a drink in the pub with many of the estate workers and lending a hand with restoration work on the outbuildings.

He was genuinely interested in the locality and in all aspects of industrial archaeology, so it was no surprise that he showed an interest in the railway. What did surprise, was the extent to which he was prepared to become involved.

"You'll not object to me acting fireman I hope?" he asked, when plans were being made for the opening of the new tourist attraction. So it was that Gwilym remained clean and un-perspiring, as the engine pulled its first cargo of sightseers up to the old quarry.

Now Gwilym enjoyed one of Betty's tasty stews and a luscious apple pie. Satiated but weary, he moved from the table to his fireside chair and within minutes was asleep. Carlo settled down on his master's feet and followed suit. Betty cleared the table and tidied up in the kitchen, before sitting in the chair on the other side of the fire. Taking out her knitting she tried to concentrate on the complicated pattern instructions, but the light was fading and she didn't want to put on a light and disturb Gwilym. She looked at him fondly hearing his steady breathing and wondered how much longer he would be able to go on driving the trains. He was seventy eight, but he wasn't the type of person who thought of retiring. She knew well however, that he was no longer able to act as fireman because shovelling the coal was too much for him now. She yawned, put her head back and was soon asleep herself.

When Gwilym awoke at Carlo's insistence some time later, he consulted the grandfather clock and realised with a shock it was well past time to do his rounds. Usually it would be about six o'clock, but he had to be early tonight. He still had to clean himself up before Jack Lewis called to take him to choir practise and Jack was always prompt.

After the last train of the day, the people who ran the shops and cafe packed up and went home. Then he and Carlo always walked the length of the platform checking that doors and windows were safely locked. He liked the routine and sometimes enjoyed the odd chat with railway enthusiasts who lingered with their cameras. Now he grabbed his anorak and with Carlo at his heels, eager and excited as always, he stepped out of the door and on to the platform. Everything was in order and probably because the rain clouds looked ominous, no one had lingered that night. He took Carlo up the lane for his walk, mindful that he must hurry. He played with the dog for a while, throwing him a stick and fighting to get it off him when he brought it back. The game was as much a ritual as the security check at the station and they both enjoyed it. He looked out across the lake and up to where the mountain tops disappeared into low cloud which alternately thinned and thickened, allowing brief glimpses of the rocky summits. Life had been good to him. He lived in a beautiful place, had a job he enjoyed, a comfortable home, a loving wife and plenty of friends. He wrestled the stick from Carlo's mouth. It was a good life and he certainly had no reason to complain.

At the next bus stop a number of school children were passing the time by noisily bashing each other with their satchels. Dave honked the horn before pulling into the kerb.

"Careful now," he shouted as they all tried to push on to the bus at the same time. The back seat was a matter for competition but Dave wasn't sorry that they liked to sit there. They were usually well behaved but boisterous and Dave found their conduct tired him at the end of a long day. He had happily offered to take over Elwyn Rhys's shift, but certainly found extra hours more tiring than he cared to admit.

"As we get older,

The troubles we shoulder

Are more of a strain

For 'tis rare that they wane."

He quoted the rhyme to himself, seeing in his mind's eye his old grandmother reciting it to him. He used to ask,

"Nain, what's it like to be old?" She would cackle through the phlegm in her throat, her grin slitting the wrinkled brown face as she recited the verse and tweaked his nose with two bony digits.

The thick hedge came into view and he braked outside Grace Jones' house for the second time that day. She waved as she left the bus,

"Diolch Dave, ta rwan. See you... day after tomorrow." She waved again and hurried up the path through the splatter of raindrops which threatened to become heavier.

The clouds had gathered again and the occasional sunny spells had dwindled almost to non-existence. There had been occasional heavy showers, over the mountain tops and the water had found its way down the usual courses, some of it spilling on to the road. Rivulets in the gutters, paused in their frantic race downhill, filling small potholes. The bus climbed slowly towards Cwm Wylfa, swooshing over the wet tarmac, exhaust pipe steaming.

It was going to be a wild night, especially if the wind got up. Dave didn't mind, he thought of his fireside, of the warm meal his wife would have waiting. Then he remembered: it was choir practice night. He groaned at the thought of having to go out again, but knew that having got there, he would sing with enthusiasm and enjoy every minute.

He pulled in for Miranda Appleby to alight and smiling he wished her well. She flashed a shy smile in return and breathed a quiet,

"Thank you."

As Dave moved away from the bus stop he glanced beyond the gorse bushes to where the cottage, or rather what remained of it, stood. All he could see were the stone walls, charred timbers protruding through doorway and window openings and an untidy mass of rubble replacing the neat and tidy garden.

17. MIRANDA

Nothing could take away the genuine sympathy that the villagers had for Miranda Appleby. They learned about the stranger in their midst when she appeared one evening on a popular television chat show. Amazingly, they learned she had written a book which was high on the best seller list. The work was hailed as a new approach to detective story writing and had already been considered as a possible television serial.

No one in Cwm Wylfa had learned much about Miranda Appleby in the time she had been living in the village. In her late thirties she was an attractive woman, with flaming red hair and a slim, elegant body. She dressed in a slightly 'hippy' way with neutral coloured flowing skirts and tee shirts that she printed with her own designs. With her interesting scarves and belts and several rows of beads adorning her neck, she was very different from the average local female. She was a very private person who offended nobody, paid her bills regularly and lived at peace with the world. During the television interview she said that she had chosen the place because she wanted somewhere quiet to concentrate on her writing.

"I have endless happy memories of holidays in the area with my parents," she said sitting in front of the presenter, her hands clasped around her knees.

"They loved it and we never missed a visit each summer. We children loved the beach at Aberfraw and boat trips round Puffin Island. It was great." Those in the village who saw the programme memorised every detail. They wanted to be able to relay their knowledge to neighbours who had missed it. Ironically, as the programme was being screened a mob of Welsh Nationalists fire-bombed Miranda's house.

She picked her way through the rubble, along the narrow pathway from the gate to the garage, which was where she had decided to camp out. They had done their best to burn that down as well by setting fire to her dear little car. Because the mini was in need of attention, she had decided to travel by train to the studio in Cardiff and to stay overnight.

The car had been a total write off, but as the petrol tank had been almost empty, there had not been complete devastation. A local farmer hauled out the wreckage with the help of his tractor and she had been able to make a temporary home under the blackened, but by some stroke of fortune, still watertight roof.

The village had been horrified by the senseless damage. Coming as it did on the very same evening that they really got to know the English woman in their midst, it was a shock of great proportion. Sympathetic to anyone in trouble, they rallied round with offers of a bed, food, furniture, clothing, and blankets. Their admiration for Miranda did not waver when she refused offers of lodgings, preferring to make the best of things. They respected her plea to.

"Stay put and keep an eye on the place," knowing it took guts, even if they did think her a bit mad to do so.

The first night in her temporary home was the worst. Treasured photographs, notes, plans for future work and even her most basic belongings had gone. Thank heaven she had just sent a draft of her new book to her publisher. Why? Why did they choose her cottage? Hers was not a holiday home, standing empty. It must have been a mistake, surely, but it still left her shocked, cold, miserable and extremely angry. But she had faced adversity before and this act strengthened her determination not to allow the antagonists to win.

Years before on the point of leaving school, she had qualified and gone up to Oxford. Her parents took her in the Ford Fiesta which her father so lovingly kept in trim. The day had been happy and sunny, her parents proud of their unexpectedly clever daughter, the first in the family to go to University. They had been quite overwhelmed by the atmosphere of the college, but were loathe to leave her a minute sooner than necessary. By the time they did leave for the journey home, the sun had waned and a hint of fog was in the air.

It had been one of those well known motorway pile-ups, the sort of thing that always happened to other people. The fog had been patchy, but in one particular spot near a river it was very thick. Apparently one car sustained a puncture and slewed across the lanes, causing multiple collisions. Her parents didn't stand a chance when their little car became sandwiched between a coach and a small truck. Her mother died instantly and her badly injured father died later in hospital.

The college authorities had done all they could to help, but her work had suffered. She found herself unable to concentrate on her studies and did, seriously consider leaving, before the inevitable happened and she was asked to. Then Jason her tutor, had taken her in hand.

About forty, bearded, lean to the point of apparent starvation and totally absorbed in his work, he had about ten analytical publications to his credit. He regularly appeared on television and was in demand as a speaker at literary dinners. He was never afraid to be different and held many quite revolutionary ideas which he was able to put over in such a way that people found themselves agreeing with him to their own surprise. About two weeks before the Christmas vacation, he called her back as the students were leaving the room after a lecture.

"Would you like to talk about your work Miranda? I know it hasn't been easy for you to settle down after your unavoidably tragic start to the term, but I should hate to see a good brain wasted." She had murmured something, embarrassed at being singled out. He smiled and busied himself clearing his desk, almost as though he could sense the turmoil inside her.

"I understand you were thinking of leaving... but I just can't allow that to happen."

To say Miranda had been taken aback would be an understatement. She admired Professor Browning enormously but hadn't expected him to be so... what she could only describe as aware. He always appeared to be in a world of his own, peopled she imagined, by the characters in literature about whom he knew so much. She stammered something in reply and he patted her shoulder.

"Come along to my room, we'll talk about it." She followed meekly, the authority in his voice surprising her.

"Sit down," he dropped his papers on the desk and peered directly at her through deep set, hazel eyes. For the first time she noticed one was half blue.

"Sherry?" he asked, but didn't wait for an answer, going to a table where two bottles and a few glasses stood. He poured, handed her one, then pulled up a chair and sat facing her. His knees were so close that they almost touched hers, but there was nothing sensual in the way he behaved.

"Now tell me," he said, "but do have some of your sherry first." He smiled and watched while she sipped. "Well?"

Miranda surprised herself by pouring out her troubles to this strange man who listened in sympathetic silence. His reputation was such that few would believe he was just an ordinary, balanced, human being, but here he was, confounding them all. She wiped away the tears which had blurred her vision.

"I'm sorry, but the accident seems to have been more on my mind lately than it was before. Some sort of delayed shock, I suppose."

"Maybe, maybe not. I rather think it's because everyone is full of Christmas cheer and you obviously cannot raise any enthusiasm. You're finding it difficult to face Christmas without your parents. That's it isn't it?" It was uncanny, the professor seemed to be able to get into her mind. She found it strangely comforting but it made her want to cry.

"You must let those tears come my girl, it's the best therapy."

"I'm full of self-pity I'm afraid."

"Don't be... better to give way to your feelings. It's far more natural than jamming the lid on and ending up like a bottle of fizz, ready to blow when pressure is applied." She laughed, he smiled.

"That's better. Now tell me, what family do you have?"

"Oh... just Martin my brother... he's in the army, abroad at the moment. We only see each other when he comes home." The word 'home' erupted from her throat in the form of a sob and it took her a minute or two to collect herself.

"Will he be spending Christmas with you?" He wanted to know.

"I don't know, it's not likely, nothing's been arranged. Miranda said that she would go home in the first instance, but because she would be there on her own, she didn't think she would want to stay. She was still trying to decide what she really wanted. You see, the house... well it's for sale actually, there's not much furniture, we sold the antiques."

"Well this might not appeal, but I must ask and you must give an honest answer. Would you care to spend Christmas with my sister and me? Ours isn't a madly exciting household and Christmas is usually fairly quiet. We just visit one of our elderly relatives, that's all. We would be happy to have you share the time with us if you think you could enjoy it. Don't give me an answer now. Go away and think about it."

To say that Miranda was surprised by the suggestion would be an understatement. She was astounded. She drank the rest of her sherry, turned away from the penetrating, odd eyes of this unusual man and stuttered her thanks.

She found herself walking towards the dining hall, subconsciously following her normal schedule. Professor Browning had however, upset the rhythm and try as she might for the rest of that day she was unable to shake off an excitement which was bubbling below the surface. She felt flattered that he had asked her while recognising an element of sympathy behind the offer. She felt convinced that there would be a certain tranquillity in his home which she would appreciate. By the evening she had made up her mind.

Back in her village, after a brief visit to her elderly Aunty Liz in the nursing home, she went to the empty house where she had last closed the door so sadly. With purpose she set to, cleaning and tidying, making sure that prospective buyers would find it clean and pleasant. There had been one or two according to the agent, but no one had yet made an offer. When she felt she had done all she could, she went to bed, had a surprisingly good night's sleep and next day took the train to Oxford. Professor Browning met her at the station in his mini.

"On time for once! British Rail has excelled itself." He took her case and lifted it on to the rear seat. "No room in the boot," he explained, "I went shopping before I met you and it's full of goodies and booze. I say, I never thought to ask if you were a strict Methodist or anything like that. Are you?"

"No, I'm not," Miranda laughed, "far from it I'm afraid."

"Oh don't be, I couldn't bear the thought of spending my time with anyone too straight-laced. They always succeed in making me feel guilty." He steered the car out of the station car park and headed for the ring road. It was a bright cold day and pedestrians were huddled in anoraks and scarves in an attempt to keep out the icy wind.

"Where is your house?" Miranda ventured. "Is it near?"

"Not particularly. It's just off the Abingdon road about five miles further on. It's handy though, for the way we live."

"And your sister?" Miranda was curious.

"Edna? She's a teacher... music." He changed gear continuing, "A small private school on Boars Hill. Know it? It's where you live if you've got the necessary!" He held up his hand, rubbing his fingers against his thumb.

"I don't know the area. I've not been out and about much. Not very adventurous of me, I'm afraid."

"Stop apologising? You finish most of your statements by saying 'sorry' one way or another." He gave her a direct look. "You mustn't be..." She interrupted him.

"I'm not... apologising, not really, it's just a way of speaking."

"Then you should do your best to get out of the habit. Be positive, say what you mean and to hell with what other people think. Your opinion is as good as the next man... or woman," he laughed.

She fell silent. He was certainly a forthright man and the last, she imagined, who would himself be apologetic.

"My apologies," he said as though on cue to contradict her. "Edna is always warning me about expressing my opinions too freely, but if I see some curable bad habit, I simply have to encourage reparation." He laughed, "Edna would be furious to think that I was at it already, before we've even welcomed you over the doorstep." He laughed again, a low curious gurgle. "Never mind, you should know me by now." Miranda felt that she was rapidly beginning to.

He turned off the ring road and into a typical Oxford suburb. The houses, semi-detached Victorian, with small, shrubby gardens, were set back from the road in a quiet street. The Brownings, like many of the others in the road, had an additional car-port, squeezed in a space at the side of the house. Edna opened the front door as the car turned in to the short driveway. She was neatly dressed in sweater and tweed skirt and looked to be very much out of the same mould as the professor.

"Meet my sister. Edna this is Miranda." They shook hands.

"You're very welcome, I'm glad to meet you Miranda." Edna smiled the same lopsided smile as her brother.

"Now you two, buzz off and I'll see to things." They were standing politely exchanging greetings but a hand on each of their shoulders urged them towards the front door. "Move. I want to empty the boot. You can natter indoors." Edna laughed, with the same low gurgle as her brother, but she did as he ordered.

"That's typical Jason," she smiled. "No time for niceties. I hope your journey was a pleasant one. I must say it's a better day for being indoors than out... my gosh, but it's cold. Come in quickly out of this icy wind." She pushed the front door open,

"I was glad you were able to come, it will be nice not to be on our own all over Christmas."

Studying Edna, Miranda realised that here was a true double image. She was so like the professor to look at and yet from the short conversation, Miranda guessed, the opposite in character. Where Jason was brusque even forthright, regardless of the effect on his victim, Edna was gentle, choosing her words with care, but no less honest. Miranda commented on their physical resemblance.

"Oh it's not so surprising, my dear, we are twins you see." The professor came in with her case.

"And just because she is two minutes older, she bosses me to death." He laughed, "Better come upstairs and get the lie of the land." He nodded to the foot of the stairs and waited while Miranda went ahead. She reached the landing as he bawled.

"Turn right and it's the second door on the left. Bathroom at the end, loo opposite." He followed her into the sunny, spacious bedroom and set her case down.

"Edna tell you when we're eating?" Then in answer to her shake of the head he went to the top of the stairs again and bawled,

"Edna, when do we gather round the trough?" Edna's soft voice answered, but Miranda could not catch what she said. He came back into the room.

"She never gives me a straight answer," he complained, "but I gather there's tea and cake ready now. The secret of the dinner hour will be revealed in due course, no doubt. See you down below when you've had chance for a wash and brush up."

"Thank you professor," Miranda replied as he was walking out of the room. He stopped suddenly and swung back.

"Good God we can't have that. Jason's the name. Jason. Don't you forget."

Miranda fondly remembered that snug and happy house as she opened the garage door beside her burnt out cottage. The place still reeked of paraffin from the heater she had borrowed, but now she had an extension cable and the electrician had rigged up a lead and three sockets. Life wasn't so difficult, especially since her local computer centre had offered the use of a P.C. on their premises until her insurance paid up. So now, each day she travelled down to Bangor and spent her time re-writing her "Anglesey Odyssey".

Jason had fortified her well against the misfortunes of life. Passing on his philosophy of life, he had taught her to find something positive in every difficulty.

"When everything appears to be against you," he said, "that is the time to challenge adversity. That is when you dig in your heels, decide what you want and go for it. It isn't easy, but you must take each setback as it comes and find a way to overcome it."

Following that belief had persuaded her into continuing the University course and helped her gain her honours degree. It had helped when she learned of Jason's illness and it was helping her now. With a smile she unpacked the few items of shopping and plugged in the electric kettle. She found a note which had been pushed under the door and picked it up. It was from Mary, a neighbour in a nearby farm who had done so much to help since the fire.

Dear Miranda, she read, Tozo had her kittens last week. It took us ages to find the four of them in the barn behind Brynteg. One is gorgeous, nearly all white and we think it's a male. We've called him Merlin. He's yours if you want him. Do come round for a meal and to see him, Mary.

It was a nice thought, a pet cat. She had always been fond of them, but her father was allergic to fur so they never had one at home. When her cottage was rebuilt she would quite like to share it with a cat.

She remembered with amusement the cat at Jason's house. It was Edna who pointed out that it had a temperament exactly like her brother. Seeing the handsome tabby dozing sleepily on the chair in front of the fire, she had felt an urge to run her fingers over the soft, healthy coat.

"Don't trust that cat too much, Miranda," came Edna's laughing voice. "It takes after its master! He'll let you stroke him and will even encourage you by purring, then without warning he'll suddenly be all claws and teeth." Again that low gurgle of laughter.

"Another time he totally ignores you, acts as though you don't exist... until he's hungry, then he bawls his head off."

Miranda laughed out loud at this, for she couldn't help noticing how Jason tended to raise his voice when he was hungry. He would demand to know when the food would be ready, shouting to his sister from wherever he happened to be in the house. Miranda thought his behaviour somewhat chauvinistic so she asked,

"Do you do any cooking?" to which he raised his eyes in mock horror.

"Good God no, I wouldn't know where to begin. Besides Edna doesn't allow me in the kitchen. It's her temple of creation, not mine." Edna who had come into the room and caught the tail end of the conversation added,

"Jason is the brains and I'm the brawn you might say, as far as organising the house goes. I don't do much more than cook though, because we have a treasure in Mrs. Cannock who came to us twenty years ago when mother was ill." Edna busied herself poking the fire and selecting a log from the pile in the hearth. She turned to Miranda,

"Jason is awfully good at locating odd characters to decorate, dig the garden and so on. He seems to have a gift for finding them when they're needed. He patronises our local pub and uses it more like a job centre."

"It's amazing what a few free pints will turn up," was all Jason added to the conversation.

Miranda had a happy time helping to pick holly and fir branches from the garden and decorating the house.

"I hate paper decorations," Edna had said, "I like lots of greenery, glass baubles and red candles. They have to be red," she laughed, "I absolutely insist." They prepared meals together, played records and watched the television. Laughter was never far away and they had a good many light hearted conversations. Jason buried himself in his books for a few hours each day, but this posed no problem because she enjoyed Edna's company enormously.

Edna ran the school choir and a few of the children were also in the choir at the local church. She helped out occasionally, accompanying them on the piano or taking a group while the soloists had individual practise. Jason said,

"D'you mind coming with me to the Children's' Christmas Service? It would please Edna." They were very glad they did because the singing was far better than they expected and the children's' bright, excited faces made Miranda glad to be there.

Christmas and Boxing Day came and went quietly. They enjoyed all the traditional foods, a selection of good wines and nibbled endless nuts and sweetmeats. In the afternoons they went for a walk to ease their digestions and thereby their consciences, but each evening they lolled in a lethargic manner beside the log fire.

"I hope you can stay on for the New Year," Edna said through a yawn. "It's nice having you around." Miranda was flattered by the compliment but protested, afraid she might outstay her welcome. However Edna's smile and tone of voice were such that she was persuaded. After all, as Edna pointed out, Miranda had nothing to return home for.

Jason disappeared for the day once or twice over the holiday.

"Got to record a programme," was all he said. Edna consulted the diary on his desk to find out exactly what he was doing.

"Seems like they're recording another series of those 'History through Literature' programmes," she said, "and he's got various dates down here for consultations with producers." Jason's opinion was sought by people involved in arts magazine programmes and he was resident critic on the monthly 'Book Review' programme.

Back in the autumn he had recorded a light-hearted quiz which was put out on New Year's Eve. His popularity surprised her because on television he reverted to the character he presented at college, being brusque sometimes to the point of rudeness. Only rarely did the human side of him shine through. Could it be this enigmatic feature which so intrigued people?

One evening shortly after Christmas when Jason was absent, she and Edna sat watching television in front of the blazing log fire. During a programme which highlighted the important events of the dying year, there was a flashback to the 'Biography of the Year' presentation. Miranda remembered reading the book about the author's brother and his battle with multiple sclerosis. It was a moving account of his determination to live a useful life for longer than doctors predicted was likely. It was also solid evidence of the truth of mind over matter, as he had far outlived the more generous predictions by several years. It appeared that Jason, was president of the Disabled Writers' Association, and was invited to present the prize. This was a surprise, she had never imagined him so deeply involved in charity work. About to comment, she noticed Edna surreptitiously wiping away a tear so she kept quiet not wishing to disturb her at an obviously emotional moment.

As the holiday drew to a close, Miranda found that she wasn't at all sure how she would be able to slide back into the previous student/tutor situation. It might be difficult not to appear too familiar. However, she needn't have worried in the least. His dual personality came into its own, successfully eliminating any sticky moments. Miranda thought perhaps she was beginning to understand him. Was it Jason's way of remaining a private person?

He invited her to his room for tutorials, as he did all his students. There, if they were alone, he dropped his reserve and became human again. Any time she felt low or dispirited, he seemed to sense it and would call her in for a quiet chat. Gradually his influence and his philosophy, not least the selfless giving of his time won through and Miranda, much encouraged, settled down to hard work and was able in due course to collect her degree.

Something in her just had to do it. She went to his room knowing that he was alone and threw her arms around him giving him a hug. She was startled, aware for the first time of the truly skeletal frame beneath his gown. But she was more astonished by his reaction, for he not only reciprocated but with an intensity that momentarily frightened her. Then he pushed her away, almost shouting,

“Enough of that, just suppose they all did it! Now you may have finished but I still have work to do.” Laughing to hide her sudden embarrassment, she left the room and joined her fellow students in their celebrations.

Miranda obtained work in London with a publishing firm. She found a small and convenient flat and began commuting daily by rail to the office. She missed seeing Jason, but there were plenty of people her own age with whom she soon made friends. She corresponded with Edna and occasionally managed to get to Oxford for a week-end, sometimes seeing Jason and sometimes not. For the next three years he appeared on television fairly regularly, but she didn't always see the programmes.

After a while she realised that she had not seen Jason for over a year. Absent from the house when she had visited Edna on the last few occasions, she was beginning to get the distinct impression that he was purposely avoiding contact with her. Edna excused him, saying that he was recording or something, but Miranda sensed something else. One evening about five years after leaving the University, she had a telephone call from Edna asking her to go down the following Friday.

"Will Jason be with us?" she wanted to know.

"Yes, but... Miranda, he isn't well, you mustn't expect him to be his old self." Miranda wanted to know more, but in her clever, tactful way Edna excused herself and told Miranda to wait till she saw them.

Miranda recalled that weekend. She remembered arriving, worried but not unduly so and seeing Jason for the first time in ages. He was in a wheelchair, propped up with pillows and a blanket draped over his legs. His hand visibly shook as he lifted it in greeting. She stifled the cry of anguish at the sight of him as she bent to kiss the hollow cheek.

"Hello Jason," she tried to smile, "it's a bit of a shock to see you in a wheel-chair, are you going to tell me why?"

"Yes, I'm sorry, I really am sorry and I expect you'll be furious with me for keeping you in the dark after all my efforts at persuading you not to hide things. I didn't tell you Miranda because I was afraid that if anyone other than Edna knew, it would undermine my attempts to live normally. I did beat it you know, for quite some time, but the reckoning comes eventually. It's caught up with me now ... I'm afraid...! To quote a certain person not a million miles away." He laughed, but the old familiar gurgle was a cackle in his throat, although she noticed his eyes were still as piercing as ever.

"But what is it Jason, what's caused this?" Then as she spoke came a memory of Edna wiping away a tear.

"Multiple sclerosis?" She mouthed the words at the same time as he did.

"I was diagnosed eighteen years ago and the doctors predicted I should have about nine or ten years before I needed this." He tapped the sides of the wheelchair. "I beat them on that one," he added proudly. She thought back, realising that he must have had the disease when she first knew him, when she had thought of leaving the University, when all his sympathies were with her. Oh what a man.

She thought about him now, as she stood in her garage home spooning instant coffee into a mug. He would be proud to see the way she was coping with the loss of her cottage. She should have been to Oxford to see him, for she had planned to go the weekend after the broadcast. However, hot on the heels of her housing calamity, had come the deadline for her next book and Miranda had not had time to get to Oxford. In any case she wanted to stay near what was left of her home, till it could be rebuilt. Edna had written to commiserate with her saying,

"We saw the interview on television and your success with the book has really thrilled us." She conveyed Jason's sympathy together with the information that his will to fight was a strong as ever.

"Bless you Jason," she breathed. "You are the best thing that ever happened to me."

She picked up the plastic jerry-can wondering if she had enough water to last till morning and looked across to the farm where she could see Mary standing under the light in the centre of the kitchen. It would be cosy and warm with a fire in the old grate and the appetizing smell of cooking as she prepared Joe's evening meal. Miranda wouldn't intrude, even though they had insisted she go there if she felt cold or fed up. No, she said to herself, she would not bother Mary now. She would heat up some soup, butter some rolls and get into her sleeping bag with a good book. She often spent her evenings in that fashion, finding it a comfortable way to keep warm. As she prepared her evening meal she was aware of the throb of that powerful motor bike again, passing by on the main road. She had heard it several times recently and she always noticed it because it wasn't a noise she associated with her neighbourhood until recently.

18. MARY

Mary rubbed Nivea over the back of her chapped hands and idly looked through the window. She saw Miranda leave the bus and turn in at her gate. The girl's crazy, she thought, when she could so easily live here for the time being. She looked fondly at the four kittens which she and the children had rescued from the cold. They were sleeping peacefully in a heap beside their mother in a basket lined with old clothes. The white one stood out from the rest, the pride of the litter. With a black and white mother and variously coloured brothers and sisters, Mary could only speculate on his paternal ancestry.

Black cats were supposed to be lucky were they not? Mary associated white cats with luck, because it was on one of the most extraordinary days of her life that a white cat figured in her memory. She could trace the change of fortune in her life from that day. Was it just coincidence that little Snowball here turned up when an improvement in Miranda's fortunes was required? Mary felt increasingly sure that he was a good omen and she prayed that Miranda would give him a home.

Memories of the white cat took her thoughts back to that period when Joe was unemployed and she had been pregnant. They had been living in Liverpool, watching hopelessly as the docks died around them and thousands were made redundant. In most of the other industries everyone despaired of things improving and there was an underlying feeling of aggression, born out of frustration and a sense of injustice. Joe worried about the lethargy which seemed to grow with unemployment.

He was used to hard times because his Jewish immigrant father had died when Joe was only three years old. Mother and son had struggled to live, without the help of a man's wage and he had often thought up ingenious ways of earning a few pence. His resourcefulness had continued into his working life, giving him something of a reputation amongst his work mates.

"I've had an idea," he announced one morning, emerging from the bathroom still bearded with shaving foam. "It's something that will bring a lot of media attention. We could do with it, now the latest redundancies are no longer front page news. Anyway someone has to draw attention to the number of unemployed round here. So..." He did a little jig and struck a ludicrously pompous pose, "I'm going to organise a march."

"But everyone's sick of marches," Mary had protested, "and they never seem to solve anything."

"This one will," Joe had predicted. Between strokes of his razor and putting on his clothes, he outlined the idea which had just occurred to him. Mary had to admit that it might create interest, but she was cynical about the outcome. However Joe was enthusiastic and he got more and more excitable as he tried to persuade her. Gradually the old magic took effect and after an hour or so she was won over.

From then on they had both thrown all their energy and most of their time into the organization. Given a lead, people had been wonderful and the title they had thought up, 'The Christmas Pilgrims" had a further appeal. Cooperation and financial help had come from the most unexpected sources. Mary knew that it was her husband's personal dynamism that had extracted many of the contributions from supporters. She remembered looking at the map and how each time the distance between Liverpool and London appeared to grow. It was psychological of course, because as the time for the march drew nearer, her anxieties fought their never ending battle.

"You're daft," everyone said, "going in your state." Her head agreed with them, but her heart didn't hold the same opinion.

As the weeks went by and Christmas and the march approached, Mary began to appreciate that seven months of pregnancy had sapped some of her energy. She had not been pregnant before and had expected to feel more or less normal after the initial morning sickness was over. She argued with herself, wanting more than anything to be at Joe's side during the march, the culmination of all their efforts. Was it really so crazy?

She thought of all the millions of refugees in various parts of the world. Did any of them give up because they were pregnant? No of course not. It was for that very reason they carried on. They had to make a new and better world for their children, so they kept on walking till they found it. Wasn't that just what she was doing? Anyway she was better off than any of the refugees she knew of. She would not be walking through a third world country, but one peopled with doctors and nurses, a country that boasted hospitals, transport and telephones. Surely, she'd never be far from a telephone? That was it then, she was going.

The square was crowded when the Christmas Pilgrims set out. They were clad in their warmest, rainproof clothes. In answer to Joe's bidding they had all done their best to find something red to wear.

"Let's try to look cheerful and Christmassy," he had encouraged. "Show everyone that we try to make the best of things, try to be optimists. No one loves a loser, and we must show that we don't intend to be put in that category."

When Mary showed up at Joe's side proving that she had every intention of going along, she had a mixed reception. Everyone understood her motives, but not all were happy. Friends and relatives pleaded with Joe.

"I can't argue with her," he said, "she is determined to come. We both gave up so much time to organize this march that she refuses to be left at home. Short of tying her up..." There was laughter.

"If I send her home now, I can guarantee that she'll sneak back and join the end of the line when I'm not looking. I may as well have her here where I can keep an eye on her." So saying, he put his arm around her shoulders and gave her a hug. Someone pushed a wheelchair forward.

"My dad says take this then. He can do wi'out for a few days."

Under the glare of media attention, the 'Christmas Pilgrims' set out. There were hundreds of people, old and young. 'WE WANT TO WORK' was the message spelled out on most of the banners.

'I FOUGHT FOR A BETTER DEAL' pronounced one banner held aloft by a pensioner. Mary guiltily sensed that she was in a better condition than he and others of his age group who intended joining the march.

The weather was cold and bright. An easterly wind blew into the column as it headed out of the town towards Runcorn. Soon numbed fingers were glad to hand over banners to other willing volunteers. Mary, the wheelchair piled high with boxes of leaflets, set out with a determined step but the cold soon insinuated itself into the gaps between the buttons of her coat. Before they had covered five miles, her knees were frozen, her back ached and she was thoroughly chilled.

They planned to reach the other side of Runcorn for a big rally that evening with the unemployed of the area who were joining the march next day. As they neared the town, people came out of their houses offering warm drinks and food. Weary and cold, many were moved to tears by the kindness shown. They wound their way to the large sports hall, kindly loaned for the night by sympathizers.

Joe made his prepared speech. A vast number attended the rally and Mary, pleased for Joe's sake, felt good. However in the silent hours of the night, cuddled beside him in a corner of the hall, Mary only managed a light restless sleep.

At eight o'clock the following morning they all set off again. The bitter cold and east wind still kept them company. Joe had distributed the remaining boxes of leaflets among the marchers. They were to hand them out along the journey. He begged Mary to sit in the now empty chair.

She took advantage of the chair between the towns and villages, but insisted on walking when they reached shop lined streets. Walking kept her warmer and she felt guilty using the chair at all when she thought of the old man who was managing without it. She surveyed the older people who had walked uncomplaining at the rear of the column. Many suffered from rheumatism, but this seemed to make them all the more determined not to give in.

Another place, another rally and another makeshift night. This time for Mary and Joe, in the back of a tea-van. Free beds were offered by the local people, hopefully there were enough, especially for the elderly marchers.

The weather grew worse as the 'pilgrims' assembled next morning. From rain, it turned to wind driven sleet and it was more than some people could face. Even a few of the more militant marchers opted out, and hitched lifts back home.

Joe, with his bobble hat pulled low over a pinched face, searched out the committee and sent them to raise some enthusiasm. It was necessary to encourage everyone to keep going. Eventually, bedraggled, cold, miserable but trying to feel inspired, the 'pilgrims' set out on their third day.

Mary's ankles were swollen and there was a sharp pain in her back. It became stronger as the day wore on so she was glad to ride in the wheelchair. The volunteers who pushed, said it helped to have the chair to lean on and she was only too happy to believe them.

Lunch was provided by the local branches of various unions, in a draughty but dry old hangar. Straw bales and stacker chairs provided seating and factory kitchens and tea vans, refreshment. No one felt inclined to start out again that afternoon, but they had to reach Middlewich by evening. That night was more comfortable. The available beds had been allotted in true democratic fashion. There were more than on previous occasions, so after age was taken into account, the remainder were distributed to those with special needs. Mary was considered to be one of these and as it was a double, Joe was able to join her. They slept the sleep of the dead.

When they left the town next morning, a weak and apologetic looking sun broke through the clouds as if in encouragement, but not for long. Soon the sky was grey and threatening and everyone tightened their coats and tucked their scarves around their necks.

Mary was expecting to feel much better after her good night's rest, but things didn't work out that way. They had only travelled a few miles when she began to feel distinctly odd. She couldn't describe exactly how she felt, just not right. Then slowly she developed a pain low in her back and it became stronger as the hour wore on. At first she ignored it as best she could, but soon it became impossible.

Breaking the news to Joe, she admitted that their friends had been right. She should not have come, she was a liability. She screwed up her face as an unexpectedly strong contraction gripped her body. Relaxing afterwards she smiled, simulating a confidence she didn't feel,

"I think I can make it to the next town." Joe gripped her hand.

"Hold on love, be strong." They were just within reach of the first few houses when the unborn infant really began to get things his own way. Her waters broke.

"Oh Joe, do something quickly," she yelled, grasping the arms of the wheelchair as her body was gripped by another fierce contraction. Joe immediately turned the wheelchair aside, muttered something to those immediately behind them and headed for the nearest doorway.

All along the street people stood at the open doors of their terraced houses cheering the marchers on their way. One elderly, kindly looking lady urged them inside. Recognising a familiar situation, she soon had Mary installed on the bed-settee in her tiny living room.

"We don't 'ave no 'phone dear," she told Joe, "but if you borrow me son's bike, you can go for the doctor y'self."

Joe like a man possessed, grabbed the bike, listened impatiently to directions and then set off. He shouted the news to some of the people at the tail end of the column as he turned up a side road in search of the doctor's house.

Mary, warm and comfortable now, sank almost to the point of sleep, only to be rudely awakened by a contraction. This process repeated itself until she felt quite exhausted. Gradually she gave way to tears, feeling sorry for herself and frightened. She wished Joe would come back.

As if to comfort her, the old lady's mongrel rested its muzzle on the edge of the settee and gazed lovingly through beautiful dark eyes. A white cat came into the room, stared at the stranger on the settee and then purring softly, curled itself comfortably in a basket beside the flickering fire. Bits of glitter on one or two Christmas cards caught the light of the fire and Mary was reminded that it was only a matter of days till Christmas.

She smiled automatically at the old lady who was busy making tea and comforting her unexpected guest. But she didn't feel like smiling. Suddenly everything conspired to bring out a bitterness in her. Voicing her feelings she cried out,

“Is it right to bring an innocent child into a world like this? Unemployment, terrorism everywhere and nuclear missiles pointing all over the place. I should have my head examined.” The old lady sat down, took Mary's hand in hers and spoke gently.

“There was a baby, once, 'undreds of years ago. He 'ad a future what was far less promising. But 'ere we are, the 'uman race, still going, still trying to improve things. Who knows, as 'ow your baby might turn out to be as great as that other one. Don't give up 'ope, my dear. Don't never do that.”

As though to underline her words of comfort, the cat jumped up on the settee, gently found Mary’s hand and licked it. She found the roughness of its tongue strangely comforting. Curling on the cushion behind her head it settled to sleep. Feeling suddenly at peace, Mary lay, between contractions, listening to the cold, windblown rain hitting the window. The sky was growing dark and the clouds had merged into a thick, sodden blanket. Joe came back and took a seat gingerly, laughing, for he was saddle sore.

The birth, when it came, was swift and uncomplicated. Mary lay, weary but content, and with a smile of happiness playing around her mouth. The baby's cries drew her attention and she opened her eyes as a pale figure lowered him into her arms. She saw that it was the doctor, his white shirt and shock of thick white hair lending an ethereal quality. The room was lit only by the fire, a dull lamp and an eerie yellow street-light high outside the window. Joe bent over her.

“Well done,” he said. “Sorry there wasn't time to get you to hospital, but the doctor says you're fine. The ambulance should be here any minute.”

That night Mary rested in the quiet security of a hospital bed. The baby slept peacefully beside her. Joe accepted the offer of a lift rejoining the 'pilgrims' who were spending their fourth night somewhere near Stoke. The following morning a harassed looking doctor burst into the ward.

“I'm sorry my dear, but I can't get rid of the press. They're screaming for news. I promised them they could see you if you weren't too tired.”

The next half hour was most exciting and Mary was proud to be photographed with her baby son and Mrs. Bell, the lady who had helped her. Offers of hospitality flooded in from local people, and there were cards and messages of goodwill from all over the country. The press had a field day. Pilgrim's Progress, Pilgrim Baby and many other allusions to the Pilgrim March formed some of the many headlines. She was heartened by the fuss the press made, not least because it drew attention to the march. The hospital doctor said it would be alright for her to stay until she fully regained her strength.

Throughout the next seven days, Mary learned how to look after her son, receiving expert guidance from members of the hospital staff who were all eager to have a share in the life of the pilgrim baby. She joined them when they watched the television news bulletins anxious for the latest news on the progress of the marchers.

On the twenty third of December the 'pilgrims' reached London. Everyone in the ward watched the rally in Trafalgar square. In front of the enormous Christmas tree Joe made his speech calling for aid from the government, so that the unemployed could do something help themselves back into work. There were interviews with M.P.'s, with people who had been on the march and with Joe himself. The rally ended with carols. Mary felt so proud, she thought her heart would burst. She looked at her tiny son and wondered if he would be as good as his father.

Later that evening Joe returned to the hospital to collect her and they both left the next day amidst much publicity. In the foyer, the press clicked their cameras as a doctor presented her with a carry-cot; a gift from the staff. One of the press men handed them a cheque; the result of a whip round from the newshounds. Outside stood a hired car, provided for their journey home by a local businessman.

"Have you decided on a name yet?" The press men pushed forward eagerly. Mary looked at Joe and smiled.

"Yes we're going to call him Chris."

The march didn't have as much effect as Joe had hoped although there was no denying that Liverpool had been the focus of government attention for some months afterwards. There was some re-thinking and a certain amount of investment, but nothing near what they had hoped for. The really fortunate outcome of it all turned out to be a personal one.

Joe and Mary's life changed in a totally unforeseen and entirely novel way. Mr. Denney, a weather-beaten and wiry seventy two year old and avid reader of The Liverpool Daily Post had followed the fortunes of the Christmas Pilgrims with interest. He called to see them one day soon after their return home.

"The sort of thing I'd have liked to organise when I was your age," he confessed with a chuckle. Used to live here in Liverpool, I did. Worked on the docks till the war came. Couldn't go back when I was demobbed, nothing left. Jerries flattened our street. I went to Wales and joined my uncle... learned his trade... he was a blacksmith. I suppose it wasn't bad for a few years, till the horses started disappearing. Well there's some around, but now they're kid's pets mostly. There's a riding stable nearby, but shoeing their lot wouldn't keep a family alive. No, we had to move with the times, so we started agricultural machine repairs. That's where I think you could fit in."

"You think you could use me?" Joe queried.

"Aye if you've a mind to move away from town life." He went on to explain that since his uncle died he had carried on the business with a succession of local lads,

"But they don't want to stay. You know how it is, grass always greener..."

When I read about you and saw you on T.V. I thought, now there's a man with energy and nothing to use it on. He's worked with machines, he's a family man and from what I hear knows the meaning of loyalty. If you would be prepared to move out of the city and live in the middle of nowhere, then the job and a small farmhouse to go with it are yours. Used to be my uncle's house, I lived there at first, but now I've built myself a small bungalow next door."

It was a drastic change for Mary and John to contemplate. They almost turned it down feeling that they would be considered traitors by their unemployed friends and neighbours. They talked about it long into the night, eventually deciding that they owed it to themselves and to Mr. Denney who showed such faith in them, to give it a go. When the news broke, most people were glad for them, so they left in optimistic mood.

Joe enjoyed the work from the start for it was not unlike his former job in the machine shop. It took them quite a long time to adapt to country life because they missed living in a terrace house with the inevitable closeness of neighbours. When Chris was old enough to go to school they had to decide whether to stay or return and only then did they realise how much they had settled and how much they appreciated the country life.

Mary sighed, but it was a sigh of contentment as she turned her hand to getting the evening meal. Soon Joe would be striding across the yard, dirty from work, but happy and healthy. Mr. Denney, showing his age, but still full of fun would be coming to collect little Emma and together they would gather the chickens and shut them up for the night.

She looked at her two older children bent over their homework. Occasionally they giggled, sharing a secret, discussing it in Welsh which they knew she couldn't understand. It had annoyed her at one time, but now she just shrugged and thought about something else. She was proud of them both, stocky, tough little Sharon with her fondness for animals wanted to be a vet! Well if anyone could do it she could. She took after her father for determination. Fondly her eyes fell on Chris. Was it true that there was always a special place in a mother's heart for her first born? Certainly in her case it was true. Unaccountably though, she held deep inside her a frightening but almost certain knowledge that Chris would not live a long life. Oddly, on several occasions he had startled them by voicing this possibility himself. Joe always told him to shut up, that it was morbid talk and quite nonsensical, since none of us knew when we were for the chop. But what Chris said only served to strengthen Mary's conviction.

He was everything a mother could ask for, tall good looking, kind and generous and one of the most understanding people she knew. When illness upset the family routine and at her father's funeral, it had been Chris who seemed to understand her moods, who was beside her, silent and ready to lend a hand.

Joe was wonderful too of course, but Chris understood her better, was patient where Joe might have hurried her, sensed when she didn't want to be cheered up. He was so perfect that at times she felt there was something almost unreal about him.

Since he was about eight years old, he had talked about Africa. He cried when he saw famine victims on the television and showed anger when she explained the meaning of apartheid. When he was twelve he had gone on sponsored walks and lived on bread and water for days, in order to collect for famine relief. Now in his teens, he was dedicated to the idea of working with one of the African relief charities. Looking over his shoulder she noticed that he was drawing.

"What's this?" she asked. "Do they get you to do drawings for homework now?" She studied the drawing with amusement at first for art was not his strong point. There was what appeared to be a stretch of desert with a long queue of black people as far as the horizon. In the foreground were African looking men in army uniform, one with a smoking rifle standing over a body. She groaned inwardly seeing for the umpteenth time the effect television news was having on Chris, but from which no amount of argument could steer him away.

She peered again at the drawing which she had involuntarily picked up. She grew cold as she studied it. Chris explained,

"Our class is doing an illustrated book on Africa's future. That's my submission." She studied the light skinned, fair haired figure spread-eagled on the ground in a pool of blood. "Who's this meant to be?" she asked, looking directly into Chris's eyes as a feeling of dread weighed heavily in the pit of her stomach. Her son returned her gaze steadily and she knew instinctively, the answer to her question.

Dave was feeling the strain of his extra shift. Rain from a sudden cloudburst proved more than the windscreen wipers could handle. His headlights illuminated what looked like the proverbial stair-rods. In the distance he could see headlights approaching and peering through the murk as he hauled the bus round the corners, he saw a figure disengage itself from the shelter of the wall. He braked carefully, recognising the dark silhouette and knowing it would walk in suicidal manner to the centre of the road to hail the bus. The figure did just that.

19. JOSHUA

Joshua was a well known character in Cwm Wylfa, aged sixty now but mentally aged about ten or eleven, he had been around for as long as Dave could remember. True to form, he stood arms and legs spread wide and waited for Dave to stop.

Everyone humoured Joshua because he was a harmless and happy soul. He lived in an outhouse at Bryn-bras farm where he supposedly worked, but no one knew better than Dewi Jenkins the farmer, just what a free soul the man really was. During the lambing which he loved, he would be around at any time of the day or night, making himself surprisingly useful and gurgling with delight at each new arrival. But when it was time to gather the sheep for market, a job he instinctively disliked, then he was nowhere to be seen.

Dave pushed the button which opened the door, but although Joshua had disappeared from the middle of the road he did not attempt to get on board. Dave closed the door and made ready to move off but Joshua appeared once more illuminated in the headlights, this time waving his arms about in frantic fashion. Again Dave tried, repeating the operation with the doors and getting the same result. There were sounds of laughter from the passengers who were used to Joshua's sense of fun. But something made Dave ponder, perhaps this wasn't one of Joshua's little games. Maybe there was something wrong. He had better find out.

Sighing, he checked the handbrake, got down from the warmth of his cab and hurried to the side of the road where Joshua was bending over something and whimpering like a child.

"Come on Joshua, I've got to take the bus to Cwm Wylfa. You're makin' me late." The words died on his lips as he saw what was worrying the simple soul. A sheep was lying on its side with two obviously broken front legs, its face and chest stained pink with diluted blood. It was a pathetic sight, made the more so by Joshua's obvious distress.

"Jack'n, Jack'n," Joshua muttered still frantic and trying his best to lift the poor animal with its back legs. He was referring to Jackson the local vet who had a house on the outskirts of Cwm Wylfa. There was nothing for it but to try and help, Dave decided, so he asked for assistance from some of his passengers who had already braved the elements in order to find out what was going on.

"It has been hit by some vehicle, I think it will not live very long." Dave looked up to check whose foreign accent it was and recognised the swarthy-faced incomer from Rachub farm. He stood on the edge of the group, incongruous in an expensively tailored suit. Momentarily distracted, Dave watched with fascination as the rain scattered spots over the man's immaculate trousers. His must be the vehicle whose headlights he had seen in the distance.

"Well we can't leave it like this anyway," Dave said irritably, "we'll have to get it to the vet," but he was talking to the air, for the man had returned to his car.

"Well, thanks very much," he muttered and stood up to glare into the headlights as the car pulled away and went past them, on towards Bangor.

By this time three male passengers whom Dave only knew by sight were lifting the sheep on to the bus. There were oohs and aahs from the school children as with much huffing and puffing the animal was safely transferred to the floor of the bus. Joshua sat beside his patient on the floor at the top of the steps. There was a beatific smile on his face, but his clothes were sodden. Dave wondered just how long he had been with the animal, and when the accident had happened.

As they continued the climb, Dave noticed with relief that the rain was easing off and soon the lights of Cwm Wylfa glowed in the distance. He glanced at Joshua who was crouching with one arm around the now almost comatose animal, talking to it quietly in his own tongue. Seeing it lying, legs in the air, mouth open and tongue hanging out, he thought it near death.

Funny chap that foreigner, Dave mused. He had been at Rachub farm now for about a year, but no one knew much about him. Rumour had it that he had been a lecturer at the University and couldn't go home for political reasons. Another rumour demoted him to a washer-up in a

London hotel who had either won the pools or become an unsuspected drug pusher. Some settled for retired spy. Dave tended to go along with the last idea for he was a devotee of spy thrillers. He would have been unable to contain his excitement, had he known the true life story of Ahmed Ali, alias Faruq McLinn.

20. AHMED

The shot cracked his skull above the temple and he lay where he fell, on the wet road blood oozing from the wound as the water in the gutter ran red. Dropping something into his bag, the doctor snapped it shut and rose from his knees. He spoke hurriedly to a police officer who in turn nodded to the ambulance men.

Like all accidents this one had its full complement of bystanders, eager to know what had happened. Police cleared a path for the ambulance as people still hurried towards the scene. Taxi drivers mindful of ticking meters and irate passengers, tried to find a way around the hold up and further down the street car horns blared with impatience. The usual rush hour crowds were converging on the entrance to the underground which formed the backdrop to the drama.

To any outsider, the many coloured umbrellas looked pretty, reflected as they were in the wet pavement and illuminated by the many lights, twinkling through the rain. They resembled outsize confetti being washed away as one by one their owners gained the cover of the subway. The commuters grew in number until they formed a coagulated mass which poured steadily, like thick treacle down the subway.

If the victim could have seen it all, he would have had a great sense of deja vu. He would have recalled the time, back in his own country, when he was an enthusiastic young man addressing the multitudes, giving speeches about democracy. The chanting crowds had surged through the narrow streets, growing and swelling, before flowing into the main square like some unstoppable tidal wave. They had been full of optimism then, hailing him as heading a legitimate opposition. The regime had promised reform, had invited him to form his own party, a democratic opposition, but it was a ploy, a cynical move by the dictator who had no intention of allowing any form of opposition.

The victim lying in the ambulance was in no condition to remember all this, he was fighting for his life a second time. A sliver of white bone showed through the dark lank hair like some bizarre head ornament. His breathing was shallow, his colour, gone.

It was to be months before he realised how fortunate he was, that the assassination attempt took place almost on the doorstep of St.Michael's a small private hospital near London's Barbican Centre and home to the School of Research into Cranial Injuries. Professor Dzukranski was therefore the best person into whose hands Ahmed could have been delivered.

When he became aware of his surroundings several days later, Ahmed thought he was back in his cell after a session of routine torture. Then he became aware of warmth, of a soft mattress beneath him, the smell of clean linen. A sense of security and drug related apathy was conducive to sleep, so it was another day before he was truly aware.

The first shock was the blue uniformed figure beside the bed and he was terrified of the outcome when he saw the man leave the room to report his return to consciousness. Thoughts of escape receded at the sight of the tubes, pipes and other paraphernalia attached to various parts of his anatomy. He lay still, but his heart was thumping like a cannon ball bouncing in his chest.

He knew that feeling so well. It had happened when he was taken prisoner, snatched inexplicably after addressing his party at the football stadium and held for weeks with many others in one of the regime's interrogation centres. Every morning he had watched as a random selection of about thirty inmates were noisily herded through an archway, never to be seen again.

It reminded him of the way he and his father herded sheep. Had they been indifferent, as unfeeling, with their animals? He didn't know, couldn't be sure. One thing was certain though, the sheep went just as blindly and with the same sense of fear. He could picture them now, like the prisoners, stumbling, pushing, treading on the fallen in their anxiety. One morning his turn came to be selected. In a panic, trying to get to the centre of the group, he received a paralysing blow across the small of his back. He fell and the other prisoners stumbled over him. Trying to stand, he received further blows which landed randomly over his body until he lost consciousness.

When consciousness returned, it was under a clear night sky. He was unable to move and a dreadful stench assailed his nostrils. His eyes were painful, his face swollen, but gradually he was able to make out his surroundings. It was a rubbish dump, containing among normal household rubbish, the decomposing remains of many bodies. He was buried almost to his chest and inches from his face a white arm stuck out of the refuse, like some obscene signpost.

A high wall surrounded his latest prison, but beyond it he could hear the noises of traffic, could sense the lights of passing vehicles. The nightmare of freeing himself took hours, for the very effort at times became more than his body could take. More than once unconsciousness overtook him, but as dawn cracked the night sky, he crawled towards the huge gate in the wall. It was locked of course, but nearby were army vehicles parked for the night. He made his way slowly through the darkness to an open truck with a tarpaulin cover slung partially over the back. Summoning all his remaining energy, he managed to clamber up and over the side. He passed out with the effort and it was light by the time he became aware of the shouts and commands, the slamming of vehicle doors and engines being started. Suddenly the tarpaulin was thrown back and the hot sun burned down on him. He expected a face to appear over the side and a shot to ring out, but nothing happened for a few minutes. Then the great jaws of a JCB appeared above him with a mouthful of corpses, a mass of limbs and heads dangling obscenely. These it dropped unceremoniously into the lorry before backing away to collect more. With each load of corpses, Ahmed fought to stay at the surface and the only way he managed this was to press himself hard against the side of the lorry, extricating himself from every delivery. This continued until the vehicle was full, a tarpaulin thrown over them and loosely tied down. Then they were on the move and the vehicle was heading out of the town towards the desert. At the first opportunity once the truck was clear of other traffic, he slid from beneath the tarpaulin and dropped on to the road. He was severely winded and he fell heavily on one arm. He heard it crack, but he was free and had every intention of remaining so.

It had been a struggle, but with sheer determination he managed that night, to stumble across the sandy waste that was the edge of the desert. Finding a few tents beside a small pool, he drank like crazy and was fortunate to be found by people from a Sunni tribe he could trust. With their help he spent a year in hiding and was nursed back to health. Finally he made his way to the nearest port and managed to stow away on a tanker. When the ship called in Djibouti he learned that they were bound for Britain.

Permission to stay in the UK was difficult at first as he had no papers, but he had friends in exile here. Eventually, he was accepted when they were able to swear an oath that he was who he claimed to be. They searched the BBC and ITV archives for old newsreels where he was shown speaking to the crowds and they also had shots of the army trucks going round the streets, picking up anyone they considered to be opposition. He made contact with a reporter who had been at one of his rallies and had interviewed him afterwards. Through him he met several M.P.'s and other influential people. An interview with another television reporter led to him being offered work on the BBC Asian Network. He had no journalistic experience, but he did have flair. Soon he became a well known voice, his opinions were valued and he was considered something of an expert on Asian affairs. This led quite naturally to interviewing visiting diplomats and politicians from his part of the world.

He was introduced to Martin Wright, a government representative who occasionally organised meetings between Ahmed and certain foreign dignitaries. These meetings were not on the public agenda, because they were for the sole purpose of trawling political opinions which were not generally acknowledged. One way and another he earned a good salary and lived well. Many thousands were still being persecuted in his own country and Ahmed felt he owed it to them, to write about the corruption and lack of civil rights that existed. The publication of his book brought in royalties and pushed him into the limelight.

Then the death threats started. At first he didn't take them seriously. He felt far away from danger in Britain and had become used to the freedom to speak his mind, but he had to take notice when Scotland Yard did. They believed a terrorist cell, funded by the regime, was active in London. It was well known that the stated aim of the regime was to assassinate anyone who spoke against the status quo. No one they warned, would be safe, wherever they took refuge. Ahmed was very frightened when he realised the threat was real, but acting on advice from the police, changed his address, cut out his social life and began to live quietly.

For someone who had suffered so cruelly at the hands of the regime he had a surprisingly innocent faith in his new life style, truly believing that once out of the public eye, he would no longer be considered an enemy. The finely tuned sense of danger to which he had become accustomed in his early life had dulled with the years of normality in Britain. That sixth sense upon which he had so often relied quite simply failed him as he emerged from the underground. Stepping out behind a passing van with the intention of crossing the road, he was unaware of the gun pointing at him from the opposite pavement. He dropped like a stone, blood pouring from the head wound. In the general melee that followed, the would-be assassin was able to slip away unnoticed.

Five months under constant guard in St. Michael's, then he was whisked away unexpectedly one morning in the mortuary van. A brief obituary appeared in the paper the following day and he was reborn, at the age of forty one and christened Faruq McLinn.

"We think it best you are to be the son of a Turkish mother and a Scottish father," he was told. "Your looks could never be pure English. Under this arrangement you were born in Turkey where your father worked for a shipping firm. McLinn by the way did exist, although he wasn't Faruq, but Fergus. You can find his grave out on Algreich, a tiny Scottish Island among the Outer Hebrides. Martin Wright was very thorough and had thought of every eventuality.

"Don't get in touch with any of your friends here. We've arranged for you to move to the country. You must be Farouq McLinn from now on. Here is your life history in this envelope. Read, learn and then destroy it. We have arranged for you to take up sheep farming as you know something about it. There's a chap in Wales who is helping."

There didn't seem any point in refusing to go along with the arrangement. Obviously his old life and identity could not be recreated. It was better to adopt the idea and see what could be made of it. Furnished with letters of introduction, he was driven to Euston and put on board a train, destination Bangor, North Wales.

As the train bore him along to his new life, he studied his life history and learned that his birth made him two years younger than his real age. His parents had met at university in Bristol, married when they graduated and lived in Bristol. His mother was a teacher of English, his father was in shipping and He went over the details till he felt confident, then he went to the lavatory and put a match to the papers in the steel washbowl, flushing them down the toilet when they were blackened and crisp.

On arrival he was met as arranged by Peter Jackson whom he soon learned was the local vet. With his weather-beaten face, tweed cap, oiled storm-coat and corduroy trousers tucked into dirty rubber boots, he looked every inch the part. Sitting beside him in the Land Rover, Ahmed found the man talkative and friendly and soon warmed to him knowing he must learn to relax a little because he couldn't go through the rest of his life without friends.

"Old army friend of mine, Martin Wright," the vet was saying. "Told me he was looking for a farm which was a bit remote and I said we had just the thing here. Last owner and his wife, nice young couple, they died in that Jumbo jet crash four months back. Family didn't want to keep the place now, so they were glad to sell. I think it's a good buy, pretty much furnished and everything. The stock, sheep and a few chickens, are being looked after at the moment by Dewi Jenkins. He's the nearest neighbour, but a good mile away. I took the dog."

Jackson chatted amiably as he drove several miles out of Bangor. He turned off the main road and crossed a railway line, then began a slow winding ascent to a village. A sign announced the name of the village 'CWM WYLFA' but Ahmed found it difficult to understand.

"Coom-wilva," Jackson laughed, pronouncing it phonetically for him as he pointed out the few village amenities. Beyond the village, the road rose steeply and curved out of sight. After rounding the shoulder of the hill the vet stopped the vehicle by the grass verge.

"There you are my friend, Rachub Farm." He pointed to a narrow track which led up to some quarry workings before bending round to climb the hill above. Ahmed could see a cluster of buildings which seemed to be perched on the cliff edge.

"You feel like lord of all you survey, up there," Jackson laughed reading Ahmed's thoughts. "Matthew, my son, used to practise climbing on that rock face. He's home now, organizing computer courses for farmers... can you believe? Everything is getting computerised nowadays and even farmers have to keep up with modern technology. By the way, I asked Dewi to collect you tomorrow and take you up to Rachub. I told him you had only seen it briefly before you bought it.... He thought that a bit odd, but put it down to you being a foreigner! I said you had medical reasons for moving to the country and that you worked on a sheep farm in your student days, so knew a lot about it." Jackson put the Land Rover into gear and continued on his way.

"He knows all about Rachub because he's been caring for the animals." Jackson carried on talking, aware that Ahmed was on edge and probably feeling incredibly like a fish out of water so far from London and the environment he had grown to know so well during the last few years.

"I hope you can move in soon," he continued, "but the decorators didn't start when they promised and the place is still unfinished. Another two days should see you right. I've made arrangements for you to stay with Grace Jones in the meantime. Nice lady, discreet, not that she knows anything. Just stick to your story. It's only bed and breakfast after tonight, so you will eat your other meals at my place, OK?"

Jackson had been unable to house Ahmed himself because with Matthew at home, it was felt that awkward questions might arise. It would be difficult to pass Ahmed off as an old friend and he could never claim he was related. As it was, Ahmed was being introduced as an old friend of Martin Wright, for whom Jackson was doing the favour of looking after him. Jackson suggested to his contact that it would be more natural if Ahmed were to stay in a hotel in the area, as any prospective resident would. However a hotel was deemed too much of a security risk at this early stage and somewhere more discreet was requested. So it was arranged that he stay with Grace Jones who would take him at face value, as she did any of her guests, prepared to believe whatever they told her about themselves.

They pulled up at her gate and Ahmed noticed the sign advertising 'B and B'. Jackson made the introductions, took the luggage to the room set aside for her guest and then made his excuses.

"See you tomorrow, Faruq. Dewi will collect you about nine."

Ahmed soon forgot his nervousness as Grace Jones fussed around, firing questions at him but apparently not expecting any answers, for she answered herself most of the time!

"Are you cold? It's a bit raw out there today," she ventured, but before he could reply.

"But of course you must be cold, sitting in Jackson's draughty old Land Rover." Before long he found himself installed by a cosy fireside.

"These will warm you," tea and cakes were placed beside him on a small table.

"Now just you say if you'd like a bit of supper. I've got a roast chicken in the oven. Jackson said you would be hungry for a meal tonight. I have to cook for myself, it's not like it's any bother to do a bit more, now is it?" He thanked her and said he would be pleased to accept her offer.

"I will have it ready in about an hour. You'll be wanting to settle in a bit first. Have a cup of tea now and I'll call you when the meal is ready."

She hurried out of the little living room and he could hear her bustling about in the tiny kitchen he had glimpsed through the open door. He didn't quite know what to make of her. She gave the impression she was a simple soul, but he felt she had hidden depths. He would have to be careful to see she didn't engage him in too much talk, although her habit of answering her own questions amused him greatly. The trouble with that, he considered, was that so many answers were assumptions and those in turn could be incorrect. She returned with a white cloth for the table and cutlery in her hand.

"You'll want to move up to the farm as soon as you can, I expect. I shouldn't think the painters will take long to finish." Grace Jones was an open friendly person used to people of all nationalities dropping in for bed and breakfast. She had to admit that her curiosity had got the better of her this time though. Why should someone like Faruq contemplate buying a sheep farm in Wales?

"Does the name McLinn mean that your father is British? Well I suppose it must" she said, smiling at him. Ahmed fed her the agreed story which she happily accepted without question, a big smile of understanding spread over her face, unconsciously giving his confidence a boost and allowing him to relax for the first time that day.

"So English is likely your second language like me," she giggled.

Nothing was too much trouble and she treated him as though he were a member of her own family. He had a wonderful meal and a surprisingly restful night, not waking until the cock in a nearby garden roused him about seven. He was eating breakfast when Angharad called and with a twinkle in her eye, Grace introduced him.

"Meet my new toy-boy, and don't you steal him." She laughed, "I'm enjoying having a man around the place." She winked at Ahmed who by this time was getting used to her somewhat alarming manner. Angharad shook hands and said,

"Don't mind Mum. She says the most outrageous things sometimes. I'm told you're going up to Rachub this morning? If you feel like a walk, I can take you up the mountain path. Mum says Dewi is coming for you, but she can tell him we've gone ahead."

"That would be nice, I would enjoy some exercise." They climbed the hill behind the cottage chatting easily and he enjoyed her easy company. Unlike her mother, she hardly asked him any questions, being more interested in showing him where they were going and what they could see. They reached a wooden gate which bore the name Rachub Farm and as they went through it he told her that although new to the area, he was looking forward to calling it home very soon.

Enthusiastically she pointed out local landmarks and showed him, Anglesey on the horizon and the tiny dot beside it which was Puffin Island.

"Beaumaris castle is super and we've got lots more castles around here too," she went on, warming to her subject, "Penrhyn is over in that direction beyond the trees... down there, see the water... is Llyn Peris and that village beyond is Llanberis."

She chatted in the delightful accent typical of North Wales and Ahmed found himself captivated by her, she was so like her mother, warm and genuinely friendly. She was what the British called a 'chip off the old block' or in the words of his own country 'a grain of sand upon the mirror'.

Angharad screwed up her eyes and pointed to a vehicle moving up the track, "Here's Dewi now. Look, I'll leave you to it and see you again sometime. Good luck." She smiled and was soon tripping down the path retracing their climb.

Dewi Jenkins bumped over the ruts in the track, his mud splattered Land Rover had the odd dent here and there. He introduced himself and walked Ahmed round the farm, explaining what the various outbuildings had been used for and showing him what was left inside.

"Peter tells me you only had a quick visit before you bought the place and that you want to see what machinery there is. Most of it hasn't been used for ages and is more suited to an agricultural museum if you ask me! We have a cooperative in Troed-y-Rhiw which houses most of the machinery we need and we all muck in together."

They walked up the mountainside behind the farm where the land had been divided into two obvious fields, separated by slate walls. There were sheep in one field, but they looked very different from the sheep he knew as a child. These had thick fleeces, short legs and rather bland, flat faces. The walls had collapsed in a couple of places and someone had strung a few strands of barbed wire across the gaps. Clumps of wool stuck to the barbs here and there, proof that the sheep had tried to push through.

"I didn't have enough time to do much, what with my own farm as well. There is good pasture in that field," he said, pointing.

Ahmed set to work the very next day. Matthew, as promised, collected him from Grace Jones's cottage, in a battered old van.

"Excuse the transport. I always get left with this old thing. It has to carry everything animal, vegetable and mineral and it rarely gets cleaned." When they set off, a black and white dog squeezed between the seats and into the space at Ahmed's feet.

"Meet Gwynnie. She used to live at your place. She's a bit ancient now, but she likes to be out in the fields." Ahmed looked into two soft, brown eyes and rubbed her head. Gwynnie put one paw in his lap and leaned on him.

"She's proper soft, that one," Matthew laughed. You can have her back on the farm again if you like, she's no trouble." As he drove up the track to Rachub, he offered to stay and help.

"I can do most things, Dad has seen to that," he laughed as he parked the van on a flat bit of grass. Beside them was a larger, bright yellow van. The back doors were open showing the interior loaded with ladders, tins of paint and the accoutrements required for decorating work. A man dressed in a white boiler suit appeared at the farmhouse door.

"'Morning," he called, "should be finishing soon. Just a few bits and pieces to do now." He walked over to Matthew's van and held out his hand to Ahmed through the open door.

"Idris Williams," he introduced himself. "I take it you are Mr. McLinn Peter Jackson told me you would be here today. It's a lovely old place, wouldn't mind it myself... you've got a wonderful view."

As Ahmed moved to get out, Gwynnie leapt out and sniffed the air. She wandered over to the gate and eyed the sheep, then looked back expectantly at the men.

"That's my signal to get back to work, and let you do likewise," Idris said and he rummaged in his van for something, while the other two went through the back door of the farm and looked around.

At first it appeared everywhere had been painted white, ceilings, walls and skirtings, but the doors had been sanded and oiled to show the grain of the wood. The floor was slate and the obviously new kitchen furniture was plain light oak. An abstract design on the window blind was the only splash of colour. Ahmed felt instantly content. He could be happy here he thought. He didn't want Matthew to suspect this was his first visit, so he suggested they go and see to the sheep.

They moved the sheep to the second field and Matthew tried to get the old farm dog to respond to his whistle, but she was either deaf or lazy and just trotted alongside them wagging her tail. And so, thought Ahmed, I start my new life as Faruq McLinn, sheep farmer.

Three days later it was time to move in and by then Ahmed was feeling confident enough to accept help from Angharad and her mother. Between them they did his shopping and filled his kitchen cupboards. They made up his bed and lit the tiny coal fire. Even in summer a fire in the hearth was welcome. They were a thousand feet above the valley and the evenings could be quite cold. So began the new phase in his life.

It was now over a year since Ahmed had come to Rachub and he was fairly well known in the immediate neighbourhood. Some thought he was 'a bit of an oddball', but they found him friendly and helpful when necessary, so he was accepted and any oddities were put down to his being a 'foreigner'. He had become used to his new identity but missed much of his old life in London, not least the intellectual stimulus it had provided. On the plus side he had found a good manager and friend in Peter Jackson's son Matthew. Despite some twenty years difference in their ages, they got on very well together and were developing the farm into a really profitable concern. Peter Jackson himself was always ready with veterinary help and good advice.

Ahmed switched the windscreen wipers on and turned up the blower on the de-mister. The weather in this part of the world was something to which he would never become accustomed. He hated nights like this, remembering how he and his friends as children, ran out into the warm rain, welcoming it with squeals of delight. It was considered to be a precious gift from Allah and it washed and cleansed everything, before disappearing like a genie in wisps of steam when the sun rose.

Here in North Wales the rain was always cold, but although at times it was heavy and relentless, at other times it could be a light drizzle which hung like clouds over his fields. He cursed inwardly that tonight it lashed down making visibility almost nil. He was on his way to Bangor, ostensibly to deal with farm business, but actually in order to meet up with Martin Wright with whom he kept in contact on an irregular basis. Ahead as it climbed up the hillside towards him, he could see the interior lights of the number eleven bus above the walls and hedges. He saw it stop, so he changed down to third gear and wove in and out of the corners on the narrow road until turning a corner, he found it parked at the roadside.

Illuminated by their combined headlights, a figure in the centre of the road was waving his arms wildly. The man, as man it had to be, for he was wearing the ubiquitous flat cap, ran to the side of the bus. Then he ran to the side of the road, pointing and muttering. Apparently he wasn't satisfied because he then he dashed to the bus again and motioned to the driver to get down. Ahmed checked his watch before parking and going to find what was happening, he could spare a few minutes. Pulling his collar up as a shield against the wind and rain he walked over to where Dave was bending over a sheep and the other man, unbelieveably, was sitting beside it on the sodden grass.

"Jack'n, Jack'n," the man muttered, pulling at Dave's sleeve.

"OK, OK, Joshua, I'll go and get some help to move it. We'll take it to Jackson, and see what he can do. It must have been run over or something." Ahmed spoke his thoughts about the poor animal. Dave looked up at him, expecting help, but he was wrong for Ahmed turned on his heel and got into his car. Hearing Dave agree to take the animal to the Vet, he rang Peter Jackson on his car phone before continuing on his way. He wasn't dressed for hauling a wet and muddy sheep into a bus.

By now the curiosity of the passengers had been aroused, so they were busy rubbing at the condensation on the windows in order to see what was going on outside. Three men alighted and between them carried the sheep to the top of the steps inside the bus. Joshua sat cradling the head of the now comatose animal while Dave put the bus into gear and moved forward. He stopped at the newsagents in Cwm Wylfa where most of the passengers disembarked, picking their way as best they could round Joshua who sat resolutely immoveable on the steps.

Dave was pleased to see that it was only ten minutes to five which meant he was in good time to leave Glasfryn terminus on the hour. Much would depend however, on how long it took to deposit the animal and Joshua with the Vet. Everywhere was quiet, most children at home for their tea by now and few passengers wanting to go on to Glasfryn at this time. He could spare two minutes, so mindful of Joshua and his charge he jumped down from the bus and stuck his head round the shop door.

'Weasely' Williams hearing the doorbell came into the shop from the room behind, his bright little face eager and enquiring.

"Hello Dave... Good heavens man, how did you get so wet? Your cab leaking?"

"Oh, it's a long story Jim... have to wait for another time.... I'm in a hurry. I just stopped to ask if you had any news of Mary Jane."

"Yes, she's going to be alright. Not in the best of health, naturally, but she's pulling through. Her nephew's been with her all day... but I expect you knew that."

"Aye... I guessed he would be. I'm glad to hear she's on the mend, she's a nice person is Mary Jane. D'you know what happened? I'll have a packet of indigestion tablets while I'm here, thanks. My stomach is playing up."

Jim turned and selected a packet from the shelf behind, placing it on the counter as he related what he knew of the accident that morning. Jack Lewis had been to the shop, and reported how he and Ted had found Mary Jane.

"Dreadful isn't it? They don't know how long she'd been there but they reckon at least an hour or two." He took a five pound note from Dave and sorting the change in the till added,

"Well she's in the best hands now..."

"I must go," Dave said, "I'm happy the news is good." He opened his palm and studied his change, looking at it ruefully and thinking how expensive things like a few tablets were becoming these days. He shrugged, thrust them into his pocket and climbed back into the bus. He was glad of the warmth inside the vehicle for he was beginning to feel distinctly uncomfortable. His wet uniform jacket was making him feel quite chilly. He wondered vaguely if he was about to develop a cold, he hadn't felt quite right since he got up that morning. His stomach had been upset for weeks on and off. The doctor said it was probably hiatus hernia, nothing serious, just uncomfortable. Apparently his way of life had something to do with it. Well, he wasn't about to change that. He opened the packet and took out a tablet. Joshua was crooning in the animal's ear and Dave smiled to himself. He signalled to pull out just as a single headlight reflected in his rear view mirror. He waited for the motor bike to pass, pulled out and headed towards Glasfryn.

As he approached the turn up to Jackson's house, he was surprised to see the Vet alighting from his Land Rover. Jackson approached and called,

"Faruq rang in to tell me you were on your way with an invalid. Let's be having it then?" He walked round to the door and saw the relief on Joshua's face.

"Here lad, she'll be alright now," he said to Joshua, approaching with a syringe. He quickly treated the sheep and without any apparent difficulty, lifted the animal into his trailer. Then with Nurse Joshua in attendance Jackson headed back up the track to his surgery while Dave paid attention to the road ahead.

There was a problem coming up because the road narrowed severely and at this point, quite unbelievably, was a parked car. Dave would have given a lot to bulldoze the offending vehicle out of the way. However, he satisfied himself by exercising his skill as a driver, carefully squeezing past without even touching the high slate wall on the other side.

A thin shrivelled creature with a face like creased brown paper emerged from behind the car. He wore a panic stricken expression below a gaudy check flat-cap and was wringing his hands. Dave stopped, opened his window and asked,

"Need any help? You're not in the best of places you know?" The creature's mouth opened and shut, a limp arm lifted, pointed to the car and a weak voice said,

"I didn't .... no petrol .... boot locked .... the key.... I..."

"You been for petrol or you still need some?" Dave experiencing stirrings of sympathy was anxious to help now. The car owner, wretched in his sodden grey suit wailed almost incoherently, he had gone to the boot for a petrol can, found it locked, returned to get the key from the ignition only to discover that he had locked himself out. Dave laughed, not unkindly.

"Hop in, I'll drop you off at the garage. Too wet to wait out there. Someone will bring you back with petrol and spare keys, I'm sure." He waited while the bedraggled creature climbed into the bus and sat down. He couldn't help seeing the funny side of the situation, although it was certain the poor mortal in question didn't. He circled the Glasfryn Estate for the last time that day and pulled up at the bus stop.

21. DAWN

She stood hugging the collar of her short coat close around her neck. She had forgotten how awful the weather could be up here and was glad to see the bus arrive.

She climbed aboard, pointedly looking at her watch which showed two minutes after five. She hoped the bus would get a move on or she'd be late getting to Bangor. She handed the driver her return ticket in silence but as he handed it back he smiled,

"Dawn Llewelyn isn't it? I haven't seen you for a long time but I thought there was something familiar about you."

She groaned inwardly, another inquest! She said,

"Yes that's right."

"Been home for a holiday?"

"For a wedding. My cousin was married on Saturday."

"Oh, that was nice. Where?"

"Caernarfon." As she had foreseen Dave asked,

"And what are you doing now?"

"Personal secretary."

"Where's that then?"

"Romford."

“Nice place is it?” Apart from Wales and Liverpool Dave knew few places in Britain. He knew the Costa Brava though. His wife liked to be certain of the sun when she went on holiday.

“Mmm. Plenty going on and it's easy to get up to town.”

He wondered what town that might be but didn't enquire further, his attention was needed for the second negotiation of the bus past the stranded car.

Dawn, was twiddling her hair, a sure sign she was anxious. She had cut things fine by waiting for the later bus and now she was seriously concerned. Would she be in time to catch her train? That car didn't help. What an idiotic place to park. Typical peasant mentality. Was it any wonder she had been glad to get away from the place? The minute she got her 'O' levels she'd been off.

She should have caught the earlier bus. She knew it even as her mother persuaded her to catch this one. Thank God there were only one or two people waiting at the stop in Cwm Wylfa. She sat forward, tense, mentally urging them to hurry up. The bus door closed... come on then. Oh no, now someone else was coming and of course the bus has to wait. They'd not get that in London, a week down there would teach them to be on time. She looked at her watch again.

“Hell, I'll never make it unless the train is late too.” That was a thought; when had she ever waited for a train that arrived on time?

Why, why, why did this blessed bus have to dawdle along like this? They didn't go so slowly in Romford surely? Or did they? Was it just because she was in a hurry, that this one seemed to crawl? Through the village... damn, now they were stopping at the garage.

“It's not a bus stop,” a voice in her head protested, as a weedy looking little man alighted carefully while thanking the driver profusely.

“Get off quickly you stupid idiot,” Perhaps the bus would speed up now. Yes that's better, she sat back and breathed a sigh of relief.

She was beginning to feel a bit warmer too. She had known that her clothes were not really suitable for the wilds of the Welsh mountains, but the days of flat shoes and full length raincoats had gone for her. She would feel a real frump in Romford if she dressed the way they did around here. She thought of Neris and laughed to herself, seeing Neris in her polyester going away outfit.

What a wedding! She wished she hadn't wasted the money coming back for it. It was just the kind of tatty affair she knew it would be. No taste, no style, all done on the cheap. No one had money around here, that was the trouble. Even if they had, they still wouldn't have any idea of how to do things.

Neris had worn a long white dress... taffeta and net of all things! Plump at the best of times she had looked like a ruffled duck, fattened up for Christmas. Puff sleeves and a gathered skirt, on her figure! Islwyn whom Dawn had to admit was quite dishy, had let himself down by wearing a brown suit. As if that wasn't enough, the two teenage bridesmaids had worn mauve taffeta dresses. Mauve!

Predictably, they held the reception in the old school hall. Apart from the blackboard on the wall and the dirty cobwebs behind the heating pipes, guests had to use the children's' miniature toilets! She supposed food was quite good for once, rising above the ubiquitous ham salad. They'd even had some bottles of Liebfraumilch. Of course the Ribena brigade were there in strength, patronisingly tolerant of anyone who held a glass of wine in their hand.

"It's a special occasion, after all," she overheard Uncle Jack say.

What a shower! What on earth would her friends in Romford think? She was glad the distance between, made it unlikely they would ever come face to face. She looked at her watch again. Barring further hold-ups they should just make it. Brian was to meet her at Euston and she couldn't wait to see him. She also wondered what he had been doing with himself for the last few days and how much he had missed her.

They had been living together for two years and it had been a pretty stormy relationship. Several times he had departed, slamming the door behind him, only to return contrite when he ran out of clean shirts. She never asked where he went on those occasions, and he never told her. They would get on well for a week or so after his return, then everything would become routine again and they would find the tension mounting for another fight.

At the moment they were mid-term in their relationship, but she hoped that after her absence they would be back at stage one. Sometimes she wished she and Brian were married, but almost as often she was glad that they weren't. She thought she loved him and that he felt the same way about her, but when they had a bust up she enjoyed the freedom.

Her mother was always asking if she had a boy friend. She didn't let on, or before she knew it her mother would have her married off and had two or three kids hanging round her neck. That was the last thing she wanted. She intended to enjoy life. She and Brian both earned good salaries and she had been lucky enough to find a decent flat. He joined her when his rent rocketed unreasonably. They had agreed financial arrangements which were fair. Their rows were usually because he couldn't keep to the agreed plan.

She peered through the mud splashed window to see where they were. Troed-y-Rhiw? Yes and there was the Golden Fleece in the distance. How were they for time? It was still a bit tricky,

"Come on, come on," she muttered to herself, counting the number waiting at the bus stop. There were two obvious tourists and two who looked like locals, but thankfully she didn't know them. The last thing she wanted was to have to make conversation with peasants.

"Come on hurry up," she muttered again as they leisurely climbed aboard, laughing and joking with the driver. "For crying out loud, hurry up."

At long last the bus started to show signs of urgency and fairly sped along the Bangor road. There were only two requests to stop before they reached the station. Dawn was ready on the steps, before Dave had stopped. She almost fell off the bus into the arms of an elderly man. Muttering an apology, she ran as best she could with her holdall in one hand and shoulder bag slipping down her other arm. Rushing on to the platform she was surprised to see quite a crowd. At that moment the Tannoy coughed and a voice announced,

"British Rail apologise and wish to inform passengers for the London train that there will be a slight delay to this service. The train is now expected to leave at six thirty."

Audible groans arose from the waiting passengers and one or two accosted a porter, demanding to know the reason. He muttered something about stray sheep on the line and extricated himself from further comments by disappearing into the stationmaster's office. Dawn didn't wait to hear more, she would ring Brian. He wouldn't be best pleased, patience was not one of his virtues.

22. EVAN

Evan picked his rucksack up from the gutter where it fell when the girl collided with him. Slinging it over his shoulder, he took hold of the rails each side of the door and pulled himself up and on to the bus. He was small in stature and found the steps rather high, especially since the spring in his knees had been dulled by age. He greeted Dave, bought a ticket and made his way to a seat.

He was happy to sit down, although he spent the best part of the day doing so. Gone were the days when he had enjoyed hours of fresh air and exercise, walking on the slopes of the mountain behind the house. Even in his working days, he would go walking in the evening, then back to supper, news at ten and his soft old fashioned feather bed. It was the bed his parents had slept in for their entire married life. His sister Gwen preferred to sleep in a modern divan.

Neither of them had ever married. He didn't think any suitable bachelors had come Gwen's way, or if they had, she had put her parents first, staying home to look after them and the smallholding, as one by one the older brothers and sisters flew the nest. He met several attractive young ladies when he left home and went to work in London, but for some reason every time he was on the point of considering marriage, fate stepped in and he got no further. After many years away, Evan had felt an urge to return to his roots, so he had settled back in the family home where by this time Gwen lived alone.

He was fifty when he returned from London and lucky to get a job in the booking office at the station. It suited him, for he had loved anything connected with railways since his train spotting days. He enjoyed travelling by train and as a youngster had talked his uncle, Dai the guard, into a few clandestine trips to Holyhead in the school holidays.

He remembered another free trip, laughed to himself, it had been one of the most mortifying times in his life.

During his London days he always returned to Wales for holidays. Often he had his best mate with him, but on one occasion, Stan suggested that they go instead to his home, in Cheshire. At Stan's local pub one evening, Evan lost his heart for the last time. Vivacious, raven haired and with an infectious laugh, he couldn't take his eyes off her. Stan introduced them and encouraged an affair. To Evan's amazement Peggy reciprocated his feelings and their romance blossomed.

He could laugh now when he thought about that sudden passion. It had completely overwhelmed him at the time, causing his mates at work to tease him unmercifully. Back in London he wrote to her every day and promised that the first chance he had, he would return to Cheshire. A week or so later, the opportunity presented itself, so he wrote to say that he looked forward to seeing her when he arrived at Winsford station. He felt certain she would be waiting for the time as eagerly as he. He could not have imagined in a hundred years, the comedy of errors about to unfold.

It was back in the thirties and he didn't earn much, so he knew he would have to draw on his meagre savings to pay the train fare. It was a Friday and he was on the morning shift, so shortly after twelve, he walked to the nearest underground station. Counting the change in his pocket he found he had just enough cash for a train to Euston. Once there, he decided, he would go to the station post office and draw out his savings to pay the rest of his fare. He knew the timing would be tight, but with the optimism of youth expected no real problem.

Workmen were busy beside the track and the train moved at snail-pace into London. By the time he reached Euston there was no possibility of getting to the post office and catching the train north. Without a thought for the consequences he rushed on to the open platform and boarded the train as the guard blew the whistle for its departure.

Panic welled up in him as he sat in his seat awaiting the arrival of the ticket collector. Boarding the train without a ticket was no problem, but being unable to pay the ticket collector was. When the man eventually stood beside him he explained his predicament. He either had an honest face, or his small stature was deceptive, for the official took a reasonable attitude.

“Where're you getting off then? I'll give you a ticket and you can sign to the effect that you owe the railway company the fare. Give me your name and address... they'll send you the bill in the post."

"I'm going to Crewe..." Evan tailed off not caring to admit that once there, he needed to change to the local Winsford train. He'd cross that hurdle when it came.

"Now, you just make sure this doesn't happen again, son. You can't go travelling around without a ticket you know. The company will take a serious view if you do it again."

He still cringed when he remembered the embarrassment of that conversation in front of the other passengers. The seemingly endless distance they covered before the blackened trees and buildings heralded the approach of the potteries, left him squirming in his seat. He couldn't relax while they steamed past the next few miles of fields and farms, because Crewe presented him with another problem.

As the train pulled into the platform, he could see one or two porters awaiting its arrival. He asked one of them where the Winsford train would be.

"Bay ten," said the man, pointing to a quiet siding, "that's the Winsford train standing there now. It's due out in about seven minutes." Evan hurried to the platform where the train was standing and opened the first door he came to. The compartment was empty so he sat back thankfully, expecting soon to feel the train being jolted into movement.

When about ten minutes had elapsed, he looked anxiously through the window to find that, of the original train, only his and one other coach remained. Panic seized him once more and he found a porter.

"Winsford?" the man echoed. "Just gone, I'm afraid. You should've been at the front," he added needlessly. He consulted his watch, "But there's a train going that way in a few minutes." Following new instructions Evan went to the next bay. The whistle was being blown as he reached the platform, so again he jumped in at the first door. At least the train was taking him with it this time! He hoped the ticket collector wouldn't come round before they reached Winsford.

He sat gazing out of the window at the red brick buildings he found so ugly when he first arrived. Peggy had laughed, surprised that such a thing should cause comment. He began to recognise certain landmarks, a village they had visited, a country pub. When the outskirts of Winsford appeared, he got up and stood ready at the door. He pulled the leather strap towards him and lowered the window. The train slowed, the signboard announcing 'WINSFORD' in foot high lettering slid by and he waved frantically, seeing a hopeful looking Peggy peering in the windows as the train passed. But something was wrong. The train didn't stop, it gathered speed. Evan, totally numbed at this last turn of events sank back into a seat. What else could go wrong? Where on earth would he end up now?

He was not familiar with the geography of the area so he wasn't sure where he was going. He sat tense and near to un-manly tears of frustration, until the train slowed at a station in a big town. He got out when it stopped and found himself at Warrington. Everyone was making for the ticket barrier and mindful of his ticket-less state he allowed himself to be swallowed up in the throng and bending low squeezed through the barrier.

Enquiries solicited the fact that he could get a train back to Winsford in fifteen minutes. He crossed the footbridge and descended the steps to the platform. When the train drew in, he checked that it was stopping at Winsford this time and heaving a thankful sigh, climbed in.

Peggy was still waiting, but there was an edginess to her voice when she asked, "What the heck happened?"

She listened with incredulity as Evan started to explain.

"Well, what about your ticket here?" she asked. "You have to hand it in to get off the platform." Evan appealed to her.

"Have you got enough money to pay my fare from Warrington please? I'll pay you back as soon as I can, but I have to get to a post office," he consulted his watch and realised that the shops would be closed, "and I can't do that till tomorrow." With bad grace, she counted her change and found the necessary amount.

The weekend was not a success. From the moment he arrived, he sensed that this Peggy was not the one he remembered, the one to whom he had been writing lovelorn letters. She picked him up on his manners, his speech and even his clothing. He couldn't afford new clothes. This journey would take all his savings and he didn't even have enough to pay for a gift to repay Stan's mother for putting him up again.

Things went from bad to worse. Peggy stiffened every time he tried to get close to her or make even the simplest advance. He couldn't afford to take her to a restaurant and she didn't think much of his picnic suggestion. On the Saturday evening they joined the group of friends he had met before. He couldn't afford to buy a second round of drinks, so with a red face and feeling much embarrassed he made his excuses. He intercepted a knowing look between Peggy and one of the lads.

"We had such fun last time when you came with Stan." Peggy stared him straight in the eye, "It isn't working is it? I thought we were suited, but it's evident we're not." Evan readily agreed with her, feeling as if a heavy load had been removed from his shoulders. Suitably financed, He returned to London the following day, where Stan had commiserated with him. In the years afterwards, he had never allowed himself to grow fond of any girl again. He had the odd fling, but was never seriously attracted. He decided he was happier on his own, living within his means, a simple and uncomplicated life. Sharing the old family home with Gwen had been the ideal solution for a man like him. She was well practised in the art of domesticity; he kept the house in good repair and tended the tiny garden. They had long since got rid of the hens and much of the land had reverted to heath. They were good friends and companions and she cared for him so well that he reckoned none of the girls he had known could have done any better.

They were both elderly pensioners now. Gwen didn't want to leave the house much these days, her arthritis was playing her up. Evan happily undertook to do the shopping in Bangor once or twice a week, sometimes dropping in to have a word with Cledwyn whom he had welcomed on to the staff as a trainee many years before. Cledwyn kept him in touch with what was happening in British Rail and often had hair raising exploits to relate about his voluntary work with the mountain rescue team.

At the bus station Evan alighted acknowledging Dave with a wave of his hand. Another short bus ride and he would be home. The number ten was waiting to leave in five minutes and Evan boarded it with the familiarity of routine. It didn't matter that he was tired because it stopped right outside his house. "And I know it will stop." He chuckled to himself.

23. JACKSON

Jackson turned the Land Rover out of the private road and headed home. After dealing with Joshua's sheep, he had attended a sick pony at the Trekking Centre. His mind was still considering his diagnosis when his car-phone shrilled, it was Matthew phoning from Rachub farm.

"Dad, Faruq isn't back from Bangor yet and I can't leave till I've seen him about this feed account. You'd better go ahead and eat in case I'm not back before surgery. I'll have a snack here while I'm waiting... I intend to make choir practise somehow." Jackson heard the laconic laugh, sensed the slight irritation. "Who knows, one day Faruq might learn that we don't all have the manăna attitude."

Matthew, Jackson reflected, had more patience than he himself would have shown towards this undoubtedly rather arrogant character who had been wished upon them. Matthew of course didn't know the true story and had taken Faruq at face value. Strangely they got on rather well, but there were occasionally, the inevitable clashes of character. Jackson appreciated having Matthew at home and working nearby. It was very convenient because the house had always seemed far too large and empty after Jinny died.

He changed down for the climb and the land-rover splashed through the puddles which reflected the weak sunlight. The sun fell in shafts between the clouds, like searchlights in reverse he laughed to himself and his mind travelled back in time.

Searchlights would always be associated in his mind with his childhood years in Nether Wompen. The insignificant village in the midlands where he grew up, was the home of a successful engineering factory. It assumed a new importance with the outbreak of war when it was requisitioned for the production of armaments. Early on in the conflict, it became obvious that the Germans knew of its existence because it was a regular target.

Jackson remembered the fascination he felt as he watched the searchlights probe the sky, hoping to illuminate enemy bombers. Traversing the spaces between the clouds, glinting their presence and inviting the inevitable response from ground defences, they in turn dropped their flares and their bombs and disappeared in the resulting mist.

He and Robert, his twin brother felt no sense of danger, seeing the whole thing as a comic-strip drama of the skies, laid on for their benefit. With mounting excitement they would wait for the ack-ack to open up. They would hear the whistle as bombs descended, the thud as some landed in surrounding fields, the boom when occasionally, scoring a hit, they released an explosion of fire which provided excitement long after the all clear had sounded. They knew people were injured, or even died in the bombings, but were never brought face to face with these tragedies and only saw these episodes as exciting.

During the war both their parents were at home every night and if the siren sounded, he and his brother were hastily gathered from their beds and hustled down to sleep on deck chairs in the cellar. The worsening situation in Europe, meant recruitment numbers had to be increased and though initially in a reserved occupation, their father was called up. Within days he was off and their mother, insisting on "doing my bit" went to work in the munitions factory, entrusting the boys to their Grandmother's care.

Grandma had gone to live with them after being bombed out of her house in Birmingham. Possibly as a result of the blast, she had become extremely deaf and slept soundly throughout the air raids.

"You know grandma can't hear very well," their mother said sternly, knowing her lads. "But I want you to make sure that when the siren goes, you wake her up and get yourselves down to the cellar... as quickly as possible," she added with a meaningful look. However when their mother's turn on the night shift coincided with a raid, the boys put off disturbing their grandmother until they'd had their fill of the display outside the bedroom window. Like all children they were totally oblivious to their own danger or of the remorse they would have suffered, had their mother been injured or killed in the conflagration they witnessed, but they had been spared that. Their father returned from the war unscathed and the house only suffered very minor blast damage.

The day after a raid, he and his brother used to go round the village in search of craters. They found a good many and climbed in and out without thought of danger, but they were stunned one day when the headmistress announced that two older boys had been killed. A hitherto unexploded bomb had gone off while they explored the crater it had made. After the initial shock a plethora of grisly stories abounded, all purporting to describe the condition of the boys when they were found. Jackson, whose life since had brought him face to face with many grim realities, pondered over the zeal with which little boys lapped up such gruesome details.

On leaving school at eighteen, Jackson had been obliged to do his national service so he had volunteered for the army. He quite enjoyed the life and contemplated making it a career which surprised everyone because for years he had talked only of becoming a vet. As luck would have it, and he often admitted to having more than his fair share, the two careers were to fit quite nicely together. The army provided his veterinary training, sending him to the middle-east when he qualified. There he enjoyed his time attending to horses with The Kings Troop Royal Horse Artillery who were on a goodwill visit.

Odd how things had turned out he mused. Posted next to Cyprus, he was instructed to contact army intelligence and from then on his life had changed dramatically. From the back-slapping camaraderie of ordered army life and discipline he was thrown into the turmoil of active intelligence work. Suddenly his life was made up of clandestine activities which led him into an isolation which he had not hitherto experienced. He knew for certain that he could not have lived in that 'Hades' of brutality and deceit, had not Jinny been there in the background, waiting, patient, reaching out to welcome him back once again to the real world.

He pictured in his mind the warm smile, the halo of dark curls beneath her army cap. From the moment they were introduced there was a mutual attraction. As soon as they could, they left the force and settled with Jinny's father in Cwm Wylfa, where the old man spent his declining years loved and pampered. Jackson had obtained more qualifications to further his veterinary ambitions, while Jinny created a warm and secure home, produced an heir and afforded her husband twenty two comparatively tranquil years.

Though from his earliest years a happy-go-lucky fellow, Jackson's intelligence work changed his outlook proving to him that life was cheap, political theory overvalued and the unexpected nasty, never far away. His life with Jinny gradually succeeded in lulling him out of his pessimism and he returned to being reasonably optimistic. Her death from cancer made him brutally aware of the complacency which had overtaken him. Suddenly she was gone and within three weeks Matthew was to start University. Was it fate or some sinister mind which decided at that very time to draw him back into the murky world he had so willingly left? Less than a month after Jinny's funeral, a former contact appeared on his doorstep.

“We sometimes have the odd character that needs to do a disappearing act,” he said in his disarming way, “not for long, a night, maybe two.., you know the score.”

Since that day he had housed the odd 'relative' or 'old army friend'. No one had stayed long, no one had totally changed their identity as far as he knew, till now.

Back home Jackson swung the Land Rover around to face down the drive. He always did this in case of an emergency call out when other vehicles were parked around the surgery. He noticed that rain and a blocked drainpipe, had between them conspired to create an enormous puddle at the entrance to the waiting room. He decided he'd better clear it somehow, before the evening's surgery, because the sky threatened another downpour. He made towards the shed to fetch a spade and thinking of Matthew, he glanced across the paddock up the mountainside to Rachub Farm. He had half expected to see his old van making its way homeward. The branches of a stunted tree almost blotted out the farm yard but through them he could just glimpse the vehicle. So Matthew was still there, still waiting.

About to turn his attention from the farm, he was aware of movement near the old quarry workings. He hurried back to the land-rover and reached for his binoculars. Matthew said Faruq had lost one or two sheep recently because the fence had been vandalised. He was unable at first to trace what his eyes had seen, but when he focused the glasses, it wasn't what he expected.

The figure of a man dressed in motorcycle gear became evident as he moved momentarily against a bare rock outcrop at the lower end of the quarry. There was something stealthy in his movements as he scrambled up the bank and disappeared into the trees. What bothered Jackson was the rifle the man carried.

Grabbing the car-phone he experienced a long forgotten sensation as adrenalin coursing through his body made him suddenly more alive, doubly aware of everything. He dialled a number he rarely used, then after a brief contact he cut off and re-dialled.

“Matthew, Faruq not back yet? Right... we’ve got trouble... no time to explain now... this is most important and you must do exactly what I say. Ring Bangor Police... right now... tell them “Operation Goshawk”... got that? It should register, but... any problems... insist on getting the message to Chief Superintendent Tierney... immediately. You... keep away from the windows and for God's sake don't show yourself outside.” He almost threw the receiver back, grabbed his shotgun from its case and loaded it. With luck they would meet on the road before Faruq reached the turn off to the farm. He was worried about Matthew, but presumably the gunman knew Faruq was not there when his car wasn't. Somehow he knew for certain this man was after Faruq. How long had he been around, in hiding, watching, waiting to make his move? More to the point, how on earth did he locate him? That was a very worrying question for Special Branch.

These thoughts were racing through his mind as he started the still warm engine and with no time to waste headed down the track to the main road and turned towards Bangor. As he reached the top of the climb from Cwm Wylfa he scanned the road below and... yes... that could be Faruq's Cortina approaching. He caught a glimpse of metallic blue as the car passed under a street light. He steered to the side of the road, pulled on the hand brake and switched off the engine. He got out and waited till the Cortina was near before waving his arm to attract Faruq's attention. He stuck his head in the window as Faruq lowered it, a question forming on his lips.

"Looks like your cover's blown. There's a nasty looking character with a rifle circling Rachub. You can't go back there..."

"I am late. I was... Tierney said..."

"Never mind that now... We must get you away. I told Matt to phone Tierney so help should be here soon." As he spoke, an army helicopter flew above their heads and on the far side of the village, he could see three white cars approaching together at speed.

Everything happened fast. The helicopter, seeing the large, black painted 'VET' on the roof of the land Rover came lower and hovered precariously a couple of feet above the road a few yards down the hill. Jackson pushed Faruq in its direction,

"Go, go, go," he urged, as Faruq first hesitated and then ran towards the man who had jumped down to offer his hand. He was bundled into the open doorway and was barely inside by the time the craft took off and swung in the direction of the coast. Jackson parked the Cortina behind his own vehicle, removed everything loose he could find, removed the keys from the ignition, checked the boot, locked up and climbing into his Land Rover left for Bangor Police Station. The three Police cars shot past him in the opposite direction as he got to the bottom of the hill and drove through Cwm Wylfa well above the speed limit.

Tierney was sitting by the radio when Jackson entered his office. There were two plain clothes policemen with him. His face was grim, as he looked up.

"It's OK they lifted him," Jackson said.

"I know... pilot reported in. He should be in the safe house by now," Tierney replied.

"What's happened at Rachub?" The strain was showing on his face. He looked keenly at Tierney, "Matt was there alone..."

"It's all quiet. Matt is being looked after. They are scouting round the area... they're good...they'll..." He broke off as the radio crackled into life and a triumphant voice announced,

"We got him sir. There was a shoot out... but he's alive. He can talk." They all visibly relaxed.

"How the hell did he find Ahmed? A year gone by and not a hint. We thought we had it sewn up tight" Jackson stated the obvious, "been a leak somewhere. Thank God it isn't up to me to find who."

The two policemen quietly smiled and one of them, looking at Jackson said,

"They'll find who let the cat out, don't worry." Then addressing Tierney,

"We'll go and liaise, sir."

"Good work all of you. Pass it on. De-briefing first thing tomorrow... thanks." He turned to Jackson,

"You had better get back to Matthew. It's going to take all the diplomatic skills you possess to explain this."

"Yes I'm afraid so. He had no idea... I just told him what to do and left him to it."

"If you find it impossible... I know he's an intelligent young man, let me know and we'll resort to the Official Secrets Act."

Peter Jackson drove back home assuming Matthew would be there by now and waiting with a load of questions which he wasn't allowed to answer. It would probably be best to send him to Tierney. If they got him to sign the act, any future involvement would be open to discussion and cooperation at home and that could only be good, couldn't it? He wondered. Did he really want his son caught up in this Intelligence lark?

It was almost fully dark now. He looked up towards Rachub and saw that there were lights on in the farmhouse. One police car came down the track, lights full on and siren sounding. He couldn't see the occupants. It was followed by a second. They turned towards Cwmwylfa and raced off into the night.

He turned up the track towards his house and realised when he saw the few cars parked there, that it was well past time to open his 'small animal' surgery. There was no sign of Matthew's van so he must still be with the remaining police at Rachub. Good, he thought, No immediate barrage of questions to answer. Skirting the puddle by the door, he went through to the surgery and greeted the clients who were sitting patiently with their animals.

"Apologies for keeping you waiting... had a bit of an emergency."

24. DAY'S END

Dave had lost count of the times he had pulled into the number eleven bay at the bus station that day. He was very glad when he did it for the last time. Going through the usual routine when the bus emptied, he was more than ready to slide into the seat of his mini and point the car homewards. He considered whether or not to go to the choir practise later, feeling more certain by the minute that he had caught a chill. Oh well, maybe after a decent meal, he might feel better. He wondered what Gwennie would have ready, savouring the delight he always felt after a tiring day, when he walked into his cosy home with its appetizing smells.

His house was on the outskirts of Bangor, one of a terrace built in the eighteen eighties. Dave drove the mini up a small lane which gave access to the rear of the properties and steered into the area where his tiny lawn had long since disappeared under the layer of gravel on which he now parked. He could see his geranium plants mistily through the condensation on the kitchen window. Here and there one of the leaves touched the glass, causing rivulets which ran vertically down to the sill. He was pleased at the way all his cuttings were coming on.

When he lifted the latch on the back door, a delicious odour of steak and kidney assailed his nostrils. He was feeling better already and a smile of pleasure spread across his features. He pushed the door open and went in.

Printed in Great Britain
by Amazon.co.uk, Ltd.,
Marston Gate.